DOVER · THRIFT · EDITIONS

The Cherry Orchard

ANTON CHEKHOV

DOVER PUBLICATIONS, INC.
New York

DOVER THRIFT EDITIONS

EDITOR: STANLEY APPELBAUM

Performance

This Dover Thrift Edition may be used in its entirety, in adaptation or in any other way for theatrical productions, professional and amateur, in the United States, without fee, permission or acknowledgment. (This may not apply outside of the United States, as copyright conditions may vary.)

Published in Canada by General Publishing Company, Ltd.,
30 Lesmill Road, Don Mills, Toronto, Ontario.
Published in the United Kingdom by Constable and Company, Ltd.,
3 The Lanchesters, 162–164 Fulham Palace Road, London W6 9ER.

This Dover edition, first published in 1991,
is an unabridged republication of the text of the play as published in
The Works of Anton Chekhov: One Volume Edition,
Black's Readers Service Company, N.Y., n.d. (ca. 1929; translator not credited).
A few typographical errors have been corrected tacitly.
The Note and the list of characters were prepared
specially for the present edition.

Manufactured in the United States of America
Dover Publications, Inc.
31 East 2nd Street
Mineola, N.Y. 11501

Library of Congress Cataloging-in-Publication Data

Chekhov, Anton Pavlovich, 1860–1904.
[Vishnevyĭ sad. English]
The cherry orchard / Anton Chekhov.
p.   cm. —(Dover thrift editions)
Translation of: Vishnevyĭ sad.
"An unabridged republication of the text of the play as published
in The works of Anton Chekhov: one volume edition.
Black's Readers Service Company, N.Y., n.d., ca. 1929 . . ."—T.p. verso.
ISBN 0-486-26682-6
I. Title. II. Series.
PG3456.V5E5 1991   90-19508
891.72'3—dc20   CIP

Note

EVER SINCE ITS CREATION in January of 1904 by the fledgling Moscow Art Theatre (with the playwright's wife, Olga Knipper, as Madame Ranevsky and with Stanislavsky as Gayef), Anton Pavlovich Chekhov's last play (born in 1860, he died six months after the premiere) has been acclaimed as one of the great theatrical experiences. A triumph of natural action and dialogue, it is at the same time a brilliantly constructed mechanism.

On the interpersonal plane, *The Cherry Orchard* offers razor-sharp characterizations of real human beings who, for all their personal attractiveness, are capable of smothering genuine cries of anguish with their own selfish tics and trivialities. On the social plane, the play is the danse macabre of a culture in violent transition: among the masters and the servants alike, and among the various age groups, lovable but fuzzy-minded and weak-willed traditionalists are preyed upon by efficient but vulgar and heartless upstarts. Characteristically for Chekhov, the words of sanity and healing are uttered by a powerless, spurned observer, the "perpetual student" Trophimof.

Contents

Characters

(in order of speaking)

Yermolai Alexeyitch LOPAKHIN, a wealthy neighbor

DUNYASHA (Avdotya Fyodorovna Kozoyedov), a maid-servant

Simeon Panteleyitch EPHIKHODOF, a clerk

FIRS Nikolayevitch, an old servant

ANYA, younger daughter of Madame Ranevsky

MADAME Lyubof (Lyuba) Andreyevna RANEVSKY, joint owner of the estate, sister of Gayef

BARBARA (Varvara Mikhailovna), elderly daughter of Madame Ranevsky

Leonid (Lenya) Andreyitch GAYEF, joint owner of the estate, brother of Madame Ranevsky

CHARLOTTE Ivanovna, Anya's governess

Simeonof-PISHTCHIK, a neighboring landowner

YASHA, a manservant

Peter TROPHIMOF, a tutor

STATIONMASTER

POSTMASTER (silent role)

The Cherry Orchard

Act I

A room which is still called the nursery. One door leads to ANYA'S *room. Dawn, the sun will soon rise. It is already May, the cherry trees are in blossom, but it is cold in the garden and there is a morning frost. The windows are closed.*

Enter DUNYASHA *with a candle, and* LOPAKHIN *with a book in his hand.*

LOPAKHIN. Here's the train, thank heaven. What is the time?

DUNYASHA. Near two. [*Putting the candle out.*] It is light already.

LOPAKHIN. How late is the train? Two hours at least. [*Yawning and stretching.*] A fine mess I have made of it. I came to meet them at the station and then I went and fell asleep, as I sat in my chair. What trouble! Why did you not rouse me?

DUNYASHA. I thought that you had gone. [*She listens.*] I think they are coming.

LOPAKHIN [*listening*]. No; they have got to get the baggage and the rest. [*A pause.*] Madame Ranévsky has been five years abroad. I wonder what she is like now. What a fine character she is! So easy and simple. I remember when I was only fifteen my old father (he used to keep a shop here in the village then) struck me in the face with his fist and my nose bled. We were out in the courtyard, and he had been drinking. Madame Ranévsky, I remember it like yesterday, still a slender young girl, brought me to the wash-hand stand, here, in this very room, in the nursery. 'Don't cry, little peasant,' she said, 'it'll be all right for your wedding.' [*A pause.*] 'Little peasant!' . . . My father, it is true, was a peasant, and here am I in a white waistcoat and brown boots; a silk purse out of a sow's ear; just turned rich, with plenty of money, but still a peasant of the peasants. [*Turning over the pages of the book.*] Here's this book that I was reading without any attention and fell asleep.

1

DUNYASHA. The dogs never slept all night, they knew that their master and mistress were coming.

LOPAKHIN. What's the matter with you, Dunyásha? You're all . . .

DUNYASHA. My hands are trembling, I feel quite faint.

LOPAKHIN. You are too refined, Dunyásha, that's what it is. You dress yourself like a young lady, and look at your hair! You ought not to do it; you ought to remember your place.

[*Enter* EPHIKHODOF *with a nosegay. He is dressed in a short jacket and brightly polished boots which squeak noisily. As he comes in he drops the nosegay.*]

EPHIKHODOF [*picking it up*]. The gardener has sent this; he says it is to go in the dining-room. [*Handing it to* DUNYASHA.]

LOPAKHIN. And bring me some quass.

DUNYASHA. Yes, sir.

[*Exit* DUNYASHA.]

EPHIKHODOF. There's a frost this morning, three degrees, and the cherry trees all in blossom. I can't say I think much of our climate; [*sighing*] that is impossible. Our climate is not adapted to contribute; and I should like to add, with your permission, that only two days ago I bought myself a new pair of boots, and I venture to assure you they do squeak beyond all bearing. What am I to grease them with?

LOPAKHIN. Get out; I'm tired of you.

EPHIKHODOF. Every day some misfortune happens to me; but do I grumble? No; I am used to it; I can afford to smile. [*Enter* DUNYASHA, *and hands a glass of quass to* LOPAKHIN.] I must be going. [*He knocks against a chair, which falls to the ground.*] There you are! [*In a voice of triumph.*] You see, if I may venture on the expression, the sort of incidents *inter alia*. It really is astonishing!

[*Exit* EPHIKHODOF.]

DUNYASHA. To tell you the truth, Yermolái Alexéyitch, Ephikhódof has made me a proposal.

LOPAKHIN. Hmph!

DUNYASHA. I hardly know what to do. He is such a well-behaved young man, only so often when he talks one doesn't know what he means. It is all so nice and full of good feeling, but you can't make out what it means. I fancy I am rather fond of him. He adores me passionately. He is a most unfortunate man; every day something seems to happen to him. They call him 'Twenty-two misfortunes,' that's his nickname.

LOPAKHIN [*listening*]. There, surely that is them coming!

DUNYASHA. They're coming! Oh, what is the matter with me? I am all turning cold.

LOPAKHIN. Yes, there they are, and no mistake. Let's go and meet them. Will she know me again, I wonder? It is five years since we met.

DUNYASHA. I am going to faint! . . . I am going to faint!

[*Two carriages are heard driving up to the house.* LOPAKHIN *and* DUNYASHA *exeunt quickly. The stage remains empty. A hubbub begins in the neighbouring rooms.* FIRS *walks hastily across the stage, leaning on a walking-stick. He has been to meet them at the station. He is wearing an old-fashioned livery and a tall hat; he mumbles something to himself but not a word is audible. The noise behind the scenes grows louder and louder. A voice says: 'Let's go this way.'*

[*Enter* MADAME RANEVSKY, ANYA, CHARLOTTE, *leading a little dog on a chain, all dressed in travelling dresses;* BARBARA *in greatcoat with a kerchief over her head,* GAYEF, SIMEONOF-PISHTCHIK, LOPAKHIN, DUNYASHA, *carrying parcel and umbrella, servants with luggage, all cross the stage.*]

ANYA. Come through this way. Do you remember what room this is, mamma?

MADAME RANEVSKY [*joyfully through her tears*]. The nursery.

BARBARA. How cold it is. My hands are simply frozen. [*To* MADAME RANEVSKY.] Your two rooms, the white room and the violet room, are just the same as they were, mamma.

MADAME RANEVSKY. My nursery, my dear, beautiful nursery! This is where I used to sleep when I was a little girl. [*Crying.*] I am like a little girl still. [*Kissing* GAYEF *and* BARBARA *and then* GAYEF *again.*] Barbara has not altered a bit, she is just like a nun, and I knew Dunyásha at once. [*Kissing* DUNYASHA.]

GAYEF. Your train was two hours late. What do you think of that? There's punctuality for you!

CHARLOTTE [*to* SIMEONOF-PISHTCHIK]. My little dog eats nuts.

PISHTCHIK [*astonished*]. You don't say so! Well, I never!

[*Exeunt all but* ANYA *and* DUNYASHA.]

DUNYASHA. At last you've come!

[*She takes off* ANYA's *overcoat and hat.*]

ANYA. I have not slept for four nights on the journey. I am frozen to death.

DUNYASHA. It was Lent when you went away. There was snow on the ground, it was freezing; but now! Oh, my dear! [*Laughing and kissing her.*] How I have waited for you, my joy, my light! Oh, I must tell you something at once, I cannot wait another minute.

ANYA [*without interest*]. What, again?

DUNYASHA. Ephikhódof, the clerk, proposed to me in Easter week.

ANYA. Same old story. . . . [*Putting her hair straight.*] All my hairpins have dropped out. [*She is very tired, staggering with fatigue.*]

DUNYASHA. I hardly know what to think of it. He loves me! oh, how he loves me!

ANYA [*looking into her bedroom, affectionately*]. My room, my windows, just as if I had never gone away! I am at home again! When I wake up in the morning I shall run out into the garden. . . . Oh, if only I could get to sleep! I have not slept the whole journey from Paris, I was so nervous and anxious.

DUNYASHA. Monsieur Trophímof arrived the day before yesterday.

ANYA [*joyfully*]. Peter?

DUNYASHA. He is sleeping outside in the bath-house; he is living there. He was afraid he might be in the way. [*Looking at her watch.*] I'd like to go and wake him, only Mamzelle Barbara told me not to. 'Mind you don't wake him,' she said.

[*Enter* BARBARA *with bunch of keys hanging from her girdle.*]

BARBARA. Dunyásha, go and get some coffee, quick. Mamma wants some coffee.

DUNYASHA. In a minute.

[*Exit* DUNYASHA.]

BARBARA. Well, thank heaven, you have come. Here you are at home again. [*Caressing her.*] My little darling is back! My pretty one is back!

ANYA. What I've had to go through!

BARBARA. I can believe you.

ANYA. I left here in Holy Week. How cold it was! Charlotte would talk the whole way and keep doing conjuring tricks. What on earth made you tie Charlotte round my neck?

BARBARA. Well, you couldn't travel alone, my pet. At seventeen!

ANYA. When we got to Paris, it was so cold! there was snow on the ground. I can't talk French a bit. Mamma was on the fifth floor of a big house. When I arrived there were a lot of Frenchmen with her, and ladies, and an old Catholic priest with a book, and it was very uncomfortable and full of tobacco smoke. I suddenly felt so sorry for mamma, oh, so sorry! I took her head in my arms and squeezed it and could not let it go, and then mamma kept kissing me and crying.

BARBARA [*crying*]. Don't go on, don't go on!

ANYA. She's sold her villa near Mentone already. She's nothing left, absolutely nothing; and I hadn't a farthing either. We only just managed to get home. And mamma won't understand! We get out at a station to have some dinner, and she asks for all the most expensive things and gives the waiters a florin each for a tip; and Charlotte does the same. And Yásha wanted his portion too. It was too awful! Yásha is mamma's new man-servant. We have brought him back with us.

BARBARA. I've seen the rascal.

ANYA. Come, tell me all about everything! Has the interest on the mortgage been paid?

BARBARA. How could it be?

ANYA. Oh dear! Oh dear!

BARBARA. The property will be sold in August.

ANYA. Oh dear! Oh dear!

LOPAKHIN [looking in at the door and mooing like a cow]. Moo-o.

[He goes away again.]

BARBARA [laughing through her tears and shaking her fist at the door]. Oh, I should like to give him one!

ANYA [embracing BARBARA softly]. Barbara, has he proposed to you? [BARBARA shakes her head.] And yet I am sure he loves you. Why don't you come to an understanding? What are you waiting for?

BARBARA. I don't think anything will come of it. He has so much to do; he can't be bothered with me; he hardly takes any notice. Confound the man, I can't bear to see him! Everyone talks about our marriage; everyone congratulates me, but, as a matter of fact, there is nothing in it; it's all a dream. [Changing her tone.] You've got on a brooch like a bee.

ANYA [sadly]. Mamma bought it for me. [Going into her room, talking gaily, like a child.] When I was in Paris, I went up in a balloon!

BARBARA. How glad I am you are back, my little pet! my pretty one! [DUNYASHA has already returned with a coffee-pot and begins to prepare the coffee.] [Standing by the door.] I trudge about all day looking after things, and I think and think. What are we to do? If only we could marry you to some rich man it would be a load off my mind. I would go into a retreat, and then to Kief, to Moscow; I would tramp about from one holy place to another, always tramping and tramping. What bliss!

ANYA. The birds are singing in the garden. What time is it now?

BARBARA. It must be past two. It is time to go to bed, my darling. [Following ANYA into her room.] What bliss!

[Enter YASHA with a shawl and a travelling bag.]

YASHA [*crossing the stage, delicately*]. May I pass this way, mademoiselle?
DUNYASHA. One would hardly know you, Yásha. How you've changed abroad!
YASHA. Ahem! and who may you be?
DUNYASHA. When you left here I was a little thing like that. [*Indicating with her hand.*] My name is Dunyásha, Theodore Kozoyédof's daughter. Don't you remember me?
YASHA. Ahem! You little cucumber!

[*He looks round cautiously, then embraces her. She screams and drops a saucer. Exit YASHA, hastily.*]

BARBARA [*in the doorway, crossly*]. What's all this?
DUNYASHA [*crying*]. I've broken a saucer.
BARBARA. Well, it brings luck.

[*Enter ANYA from her room.*]

ANYA. We must tell mamma that Peter's here.
BARBARA. I've told them not to wake him.
ANYA [*thoughtfully*]. It's just six years since papa died. And only a month afterwards poor little Grisha was drowned in the river; my pretty little brother, only seven years old! It was too much for mamma; she ran away, ran away without looking back. [*Shuddering.*] How well I can understand her, if only she knew! [*A pause.*] Peter Trophímof was Grisha's tutor; he might remind her.

[*Enter FIRS in long coat and white waistcoat.*]

FIRS [*going over to the coffee-pot, anxiously*]. My mistress is going to take coffee here. [*Putting on white gloves.*] Is the coffee ready? [*Sternly, to DUNYASHA.*] Here, girl, where's the cream?
DUNYASHA. Oh, dear! Oh dear!

[*Exit DUNYASHA, hastily.*]

FIRS [*bustling about the coffee-pot*]. Ah, you . . . job-lot! [*Mumbling to himself.*] She's come back from Paris. The master went to Paris once in a post-chaise. [*Laughing.*]
BARBARA. What is it, Firs?
FIRS. I beg your pardon? [*Joyfully.*] My mistress has come home; at last I've seen her. Now I'm ready to die.

[*He cries with joy. Enter MADAME RANEVSKY, LOPAKHIN, GAYEF and PISHTCHIK; PISHTCHIK in Russian breeches and coat of fine cloth. GAYEF as he enters makes gestures as if playing billiards.*]

MADAME RANEVSKY. What was the expression? Let me see. 'I'll put the red in the corner pocket; double into the middle——'

GAYEF. I'll chip the red in the right-hand top. Once upon a time. Lyuba, when we were children, we used to sleep here side by side in two little cots, and now I'm fifty-one, and can't bring myself to believe it.

LOPAKHIN. Yes; time flies.

GAYEF. Who's that?

LOPAKHIN. Time flies. I say.

GAYEF. There's a smell of patchouli!

ANYA. I am going to bed. Good-night, mamma. [*Kissing her mother.*]

MADAME RANEVSKY. My beloved little girl! [*Kissing her hands.*] Are you glad you're home again? I can't come to my right senses.

ANYA. Good-night, uncle.

GAYEF [*kissing her face and hands*]. God bless you, little Anya. How like your mother you are! [*To* MADAME RANEVSKY.] You were just such another girl at her age, Lyuba.

[ANYA *shakes hands with* LOPAKHIN *and* SIMEONOF-PISHTCHIK *and exit, shutting her bedroom door behind her.*]

MADAME RANEVSKY. She's very, very tired.

PISHTCHIK. It must have been a long journey.

BARBARA [*to* LOPAKHIN *and* PISHTCHIK]. Well, gentlemen, it's past two; time you were off.

MADAME RANEVSKY [*laughing*]. You haven't changed a bit, Barbara! [*Drawing her to herself and kissing her.*] I'll just finish my coffee, then we'll all go. [FIRS *puts a footstool under her feet.*] Thank you, friend. I'm used to my coffee. I drink it day and night. Thank you, you dear old man. [*Kissing* FIRS.]

BARBARA. I'll go and see if they've got all the luggage. [*Exit* BARBARA.]

MADAME RANEVSKY. Can it be me that's sitting here? [*Laughing.*] I want to jump and wave my arms about. [*Pausing and covering her face.*] Surely I must be dreaming! God knows I love my country. I love it tenderly. I couldn't see out of the window from the train, I was crying so. [*Crying.*] However, I must drink my coffee. Thank you, Firs; thank you, dear old man. I'm so glad to find you still alive.

FIRS. The day before yesterday.

GAYEF. He's hard of hearing.

LOPAKHIN. I've got to be off for Kharkof by the five o'clock train. Such a nuisance! I wanted to stay and look at you and talk to you. You're as splendid as you always were.

PISHTCHIK [*sighing heavily*]. Handsomer than ever and dressed like a Parisian . . . perish my waggon and all its wheels!

LOPAKHIN. Your brother, Leoníd Andréyitch, says I'm a snob, a money-grubber. He can say what he likes. I don't care a hang. Only I want you to believe in me as you used to; I want your wonderful, touching eyes to look at me as they used to. Merciful God in heaven! My father was your father's serf, and your grandfather's serf before him; but you, you did so much for me in the old days that I've forgotten everything, and I love you like a sister—more than a sister.

MADAME RANEVSKY. I can't sit still! I can't do it! [*Jumping up and walking about in great agitation.*] This happiness is more than I can bear. Laugh at me! I am a fool! [*Kissing a cupboard.*] My darling old cupboard! [*Caressing a table.*] My dear little table!

GAYEF. Nurse is dead since you went away.

MADAME RANEVSKY [*sitting down and drinking coffee*]. Yes, Heaven rest her soul. They wrote and told me.

GAYEF. And Anastási is dead. Squint-eyed Peter has left us and works in the town at the Police Inspector's now.

[GAYEF *takes out a box of sugar candy from his pocket, and begins to eat it.*]

PISHTCHIK. My daughter Dáshenka sent her compliments.

LOPAKHIN. I long to say something charming and delightful to you. [*Looking at his watch.*] I'm just off; there's no time to talk. Well, yes, I'll put it in two or three words. You know that your cherry orchard is going to be sold to pay the mortgage: the sale is fixed for the twenty-second of August; but don't you be uneasy, my dear lady; sleep peacefully; there's a way out of it. This is my plan. Listen to me carefully. Your property is only fifteen miles from the town; the railway runs close beside it; and if only you will cut up the cherry orchard and the land along the river into building lots and let it off on lease for villas, you will get at least two thousand five hundred pounds a year out of it.

GAYEF. Come, come! What rubbish you're talking!

MADAME RANEVSKY. I don't quite understand what you mean, Yermolái Alexéyitch.

LOPAKHIN. You will get a pound a year at least for every acre from the tenants, and if you advertise the thing at once, I am ready to bet whatever you like, by the autumn you won't have a clod of that earth left on your hands. It'll all be snapped up. In two words, I congratulate you; you are saved. It's a first-class site, with a good deep river. Only of course you will have to put it in order and clear the ground; you will have to pull down all the old buildings—this house, for instance, which is no longer fit for anything; you'll have to cut down the cherry orchard. . . .

MADAME RANEVSKY. Cut down the cherry orchard! Excuse me, but you don't know what you're talking about. If there is one thing that's interesting, remarkable in fact, in the whole province, it's our cherry orchard.

LOPAKHIN. There's nothing remarkable about the orchard except that it's a very big one. It only bears once every two years, and then you don't know what to do with the fruit. Nobody wants to buy it.

GAYEF. Our cherry orchard is mentioned in Andréyevsky's Encyclopaedia.

LOPAKHIN [looking at his watch]. If we don't make up our minds or think of any way, on the twenty-second of August the cherry orchard and the whole property will be sold by auction. Come, make up your mind! There's no other way out of it, I swear—absolutely none.

FIRS. In the old days, forty or fifty years ago, they used to dry the cherries and soak 'em and pickle 'em, and make jam of 'em; and the dried cherries . . .

GAYEF. Shut up, Firs.

FIRS. The dried cherries used to be sent in waggons to Moscow and Kharkof. A heap of money! The dried cherries were soft and juicy and sweet and sweet-smelling then. They knew some way in those days.

MADAME RANEVSKY. And why don't they do it now?

FIRS. They've forgotten. Nobody remembers how to do it.

PISHTCHIK [to MADAME RANEVSKY]. What about Paris? How did you get on? Did you eat frogs?

MADAME RANEVSKY. Crocodiles.

PISHTCHIK. You don't say so! Well, I never!

LOPAKHIN. Until a little while ago there was nothing but gentry and peasants in the villages; but now villa residents have made their appearance. All the towns, even the little ones, are surrounded by villas now. In another twenty years the villa resident will have multiplied like anything. At present he only sits and drinks tea on his verandah, but it is quite likely that he will soon take to cultivating his three acres of land, and then your old cherry orchard will become fruitful, rich and happy. . . .

GAYEF [angry]. What gibberish!

[Enter BARBARA and YASHA.]

BARBARA [taking out a key and noisily unlocking an old-fashioned cupboard]. There are two telegrams for you, mamma. Here they are.

MADAME RANEVSKY [tearing them up without reading them]. They're from Paris. I've done with Paris.

GAYEF. Do you know how old this cupboard is, Lyuba? A week ago I pulled out the bottom drawer and saw a date burnt in it. That cupboard was made exactly a hundred years ago. What do you think of that, eh? We might celebrate its jubilee. It's only an inanimate thing, but for all that it's a historic cupboard.

PISHTCHIK [*astonished*]. A hundred years? Well, I never!

GAYEF [*touching the cupboard*]. Yes, it's a wonderful thing. . . . Beloved and venerable cupboard; honour and glory to your existence, which for more than a hundred years has been directed to the noble ideals of justice and virtue. Your silent summons to profitable labour has never weakened in all these hundred years. [*Crying.*] You have upheld the courage of succeeding generations of our human kind; you have upheld faith in a better future and cherished in us ideals of goodness and social consciousness. [*A pause.*]

LOPAKHIN. Yes. . . .

MADAME RANEVSKY. You haven't changed, Leoníd.

GAYEF [*embarrassed*]. Off the white in the corner, chip the red in the middle pocket!

LOPAKHIN [*looking at his watch*]. Well, I must be off.

YASHA [*handing a box to* MADAME RANEVSKY]. Perhaps you'll take your pills now.

PISHTCHIK. You oughtn't to take medicine, dear lady. It does you neither good nor harm. Give them here, my friend. [*He empties all the pills into the palm of his hand, blows on them, puts them in his mouth and swallows them down with a draught of quass.*] There!

MADAME RANEVSKY [*alarmed*]. Have you gone off your head?

PISHTCHIK. I've taken all the pills.

LOPAKHIN. Greedy fellow! [*Everyone laughs.*]

FIRS [*mumbling*]. They were here in Easter week and finished off a gallon of pickled gherkins.

MADAME RANEVSKY. What's he talking about?

BARBARA. He's been mumbling like that these three years. We've got used to it.

YASHA. Advancing age.

[CHARLOTTE *crosses in a white frock, very thin, tightly laced, with a lorgnette at her waist.*]

LOPAKHIN. Excuse me, Charlotte Ivánovna, I've not paid my respects to you yet. [*He prepares to kiss her hand.*]

CHARLOTTE [*drawing her hand away*]. If one allows you to kiss one's hand, you will want to kiss one's elbow next, and then one's shoulder.

LOPAKHIN. I'm having no luck today. [*All laugh.*] Charlotte Ivánovna, do us a conjuring trick.

MADAME RANEVSKY. Charlotte, do do us a conjuring trick.

CHARLOTTE. No, thank you. I'm going to bed.

[*Exit* CHARLOTTE.]

LOPAKHIN. We shall meet again in three weeks. [*Kissing* MADAME RANEVSKY'S *hand.*] Meanwhile, good-bye. I must be off. [*To* GAYEF.] So-long. [*Kissing* PISHTCHIK.] Ta-ta. [*Shaking hands with* BARBARA, *then with* FIRS *and* YASHA.] I hate having to go. [*To* MADAME RANEVSKY.] If you make up your mind about the villas, let me know, and I'll raise you five thousand pounds at once. Think it over seriously.

BARBARA [*angrily*]. For heaven's sake do go!

LOPAKHIN. I'm going, I'm going.

[*Exit* LOPAKHIN.]

GAYEF. Snob! . . . However, *pardon!* Barbara's going to marry him; he's Barbara's young man.

BARBARA. You talk too much, uncle.

MADAME RANEVSKY. Why, Barbara, I shall be very glad. He's a nice man.

PISHTCHIK. Not a doubt about it. . . . A most worthy individual. My Dáshenka, she says . . . oh, she says . . . lots of things. [*Snoring and waking up again at once.*] By the by, dear lady, can you lend me twenty-five pounds? I've got to pay the interest on my mortgage to-morrow.

BARBARA [*alarmed*]. We can't! we can't!

MADAME RANEVSKY. It really is a fact that I haven't any money.

PISHTCHIK. I'll find it somewhere. [*Laughing.*] I never lose hope. Last time I thought: 'Now I really am done for, I'm a ruined man,' when behold, they ran a railway over my land and paid me compensation. And so it'll be again; something will happen, if not today, then to-morrow. Dáshenka may win the twenty-thousand-pound prize; she's got a ticket in the lottery.

MADAME RANEVSKY. The coffee's finished. Let's go to bed.

FIRS [*brushing* GAYEF'S *clothes, admonishingly*]. You've put on the wrong trousers again. Whatever am I to do with you?

BARBARA [*softly*]. Anya is asleep. [*She opens the window quietly.*] The sun's up already; it isn't cold now. Look, mamma, how lovely the trees are. Heavens! what a sweet air! The starlings are singing!

GAYEF [*opening the other window*]. The orchard is all white. You've not forgotten it, Lyuba? This long avenue going straight on, straight on, like a ribbon between the trees? It shines like silver on moonlight nights. Do you remember? You've not forgotten?

MADAME RANEVSKY [*looking out into the garden*]. Oh, my childhood, my pure and happy childhood! I used to sleep in this nursery. I used to look out from here into the garden. Happiness awoke with me every morning! and the orchard was just the same then as it is now; nothing is altered. [*Laughing with joy.*] It is all white, all white! Oh, my cherry orchard! After the dark and stormy autumn and the frosts of winter you are young again and full of happiness; the angels of heaven have not abandoned you. Oh! if only I could free my neck and shoulders from the stone that weighs them down! If only I could forget my past!

GAYEF. Yes; and this orchard will be sold to pay our debts, however impossible it may seem. . . .

MADAME RANEVSKY. Look! There's mamma walking in the orchard . . . in a white frock! [*Laughing with joy.*] There she is!

GAYEF. Where?

BARBARA. Heaven help you!

MADAME RANEVSKY. There's no one there, really. It only looked like it; there on the right where the path turns down to the summer-house; there's a white tree that leans over and looks like a woman. [*Enter* TROPHIMOF *in a shabby student uniform and spectacles.*] What a wonderful orchard, with its white masses of blossom and the blue sky above!

TROPHIMOF. Lyubóf Andréyevna! [*She looks round at him.*] I only want to say, 'How do you do,' and go away at once. [*Kissing her hand eagerly.*] I was told to wait till the morning, but I hadn't the patience.

[MADAME RANEVSKY *looks at him in astonishment.*]

BARBARA [*crying*]. This is Peter Trophímof.

TROPHIMOF. Peter Trophímof; I was Grisha's tutor, you know. Have I really altered so much?

[MADAME RANEVSKY *embraces him and cries softly.*]

GAYEF. Come, come, that's enough, Lyuba!

BARBARA [*crying*]. I told you to wait till to-morrow, you know, Peter.

MADAME RANEVSKY. My little Grisha! My little boy! Grisha . . . my son. . . .

BARBARA. It can't be helped, mamma. It was the will of God.

TROPHIMOF [*gently, crying*]. There, there!

MADAME RANEVSKY [*crying*]. He was drowned. My little boy was drowned. Why? What was the use of that, my dear? [*In a softer voice.*] Anya's asleep in there, and I am speaking so loud, and making a noise. . . . But tell me, Peter, why have you grown so ugly? Why have you grown so old?

TROPHIMOF. An old woman in the train called me a 'mouldy gentleman.'

MADAME RANEVSKY. You were quite a boy then, a dear little student, and now your hair's going and you wear spectacles. Are you really still a student? [*Going towards the door.*]

TROPHIMOF. Yes, I expect I shall be a perpetual student.

MADAME RANEVSKY [*kissing her brother and then* BARBARA]. Well, go to bed. You've grown old too, Leoníd.

PISHTCHIK [*following her*]. Yes, yes; time for bed. Oh, oh, my gout! I'll stay the night here. Don't forget, Lyubóf Andréyevna, my angel, to-morrow morning . . . twenty-five.

GAYEF. He's still on the same string.

PISHTCHIK. Twenty-five . . . to pay the interest on my mortgage.

MADAME RANEVSKY. I haven't any money, my friend.

PISHTCHIK. I'll pay you back, dear lady. It's a trifling sum.

MADAME RANEVSKY. Well, well, Leoníd will give it to you. Let him have it, Leoníd.

GAYEF [*ironical*]. I'll give it him right enough! Hold your pocket wide!

MADAME RANEVSKY. It can't be helped. . . . He needs it. He'll pay it back.

[*Exeunt* MADAME RANEVSKY, TROPHIMOF, PISHTCHIK *and* FIRS. GAYEF, BARBARA *and* YASHA *remain.*]

GAYEF. My sister hasn't lost her old habit of scattering the money. [*To* YASHA.] Go away, my lad! You smell of chicken.

YASHA [*laughing*]. You're just the same as you always were, Leoníd Andréyevitch!

GAYEF. Who's that? [*To* BARBARA.] What does he say?

BARBARA [*to* YASHA]. Your mother's come up from the village. She's been waiting for you since yesterday in the servants' hall. She wants to see you.

YASHA. What a nuisance she is!

BARBARA. You wicked, unnatural son!

YASHA. Well, what do I want with her? She might just as well have waited till to-morrow.

[*Exit* YASHA.]

BARBARA. Mamma is just like she used to be; she hasn't changed a bit. If she had her way, she'd give away everything she has.

GAYEF. Yes. [*A pause.*] If people recommend very many cures for an illness, that means that the illness is incurable. I think and think, I batter my brains; I know of many remedies, very many, and that means really that there is none. How nice it would be to get a fortune left one by somebody! How nice it would be if Anya could marry a very rich man! How nice it would be to go to Yaroslav and try my luck with my aunt the Countess. My aunt is very, very rich, you know.

BARBARA [*crying softly*]. If only God would help us!

GAYEF. Don't howl! My aunt is very rich, but she does not like us. In the first place, my sister married a solicitor, not a nobleman. [ANYA *appears in the doorway.*] She married a man who was not a nobleman, and it's no good pretending that she has led a virtuous life. She's a dear, kind, charming creature, and I love her very much, but whatever mitigating circumstances one may find for her, there's no getting round it that she's a sinful woman. You can see it in her every gesture.

BARBARA [*whispering*]. Anya is standing in the door!

GAYEF. Who's that? [*A pause.*] It's very odd, something's got into my right eye. I can't see properly out of it. Last Thursday when I was down at the District Court . . .

[ANYA *comes down.*]

BARBARA. Why aren't you asleep, Anya?

ANYA. I can't sleep. It's no good trying.

GAYEF. My little pet! [*Kissing* ANYA's *hands and face.*] My little girl! [*Crying.*] You're not my niece; you're my angel; you're my everything. Trust me, trust me. . . .

ANYA. I do trust you, uncle. Everyone loves you, everyone respects you; but dear, dear uncle, you ought to hold your tongue, only to hold your tongue. What were you saying just now about mamma? about your own sister? What was the good of saying that?

GAYEF. Yes, yes. [*Covering his face with her hand.*] You're quite right; it was awful of me! Lord, Lord! save me from myself! And a little while ago I made a speech over a cupboard. What a stupid thing to do! As soon as I had done it, I knew it was stupid.

BARBARA. Yes, really, uncle. You ought to hold your tongue. Say nothing; that's all that's wanted.

ANYA. If only you would hold your tongue, you'd be so much happier!

GAYEF. I will! I will! [*Kissing* ANYA's *and* BARBARA's *hands.*] I'll hold my tongue. But there's one thing I must say; it's business. Last Thursday, when I was down at the District Court, a lot of us were there together, we began to talk about this and that, one thing and another, and it seems I could arrange a loan on note of hand to pay the interest into the bank.

BARBARA. If only Heaven would help us!

GAYEF. I'll go on Tuesday and talk it over again. [*To* BARBARA.] Don't howl! [*To* ANYA.] Your mamma shall have a talk with Lopákhin. Of course he won't refuse her. And as soon as you are rested you must go to see your grandmother, the Countess, at Yaroslav. We'll operate from three points, and the trick is done. We'll pay the interest, I'm certain of it. [*Taking sugar candy.*] I swear on my honour, or whatever you will, the property shall not be sold. [*Excitedly.*] I swear by my hope of eternal happiness! There's my hand on it. Call me a base, dishonourable man if I let it go to auction. I swear by my whole being.

ANYA [*calm again and happy*]. What a dear you are, uncle, and how clever! [*Embraces him.*] Now I'm easy again. I'm easy again! I'm happy!

[*Enter* FIRS.]

FIRS [*reproachfully*]. Leoníd Andréyevitch, have you no fear of God? When are you going to bed?

GAYEF. I'm just off—just off. You get along, Firs. I'll undress myself all right. Come, children, bye-bye! Details to-morrow, but now let's go to bed. [*Kissing* ANYA *and* BARBARA.] I'm a good Liberal, a man of the eighties. People abuse the eighties, but I think that I may say I've suffered something for my convictions in my time. It's not for nothing that the peasants love me. We ought to know the peasants; we ought to know with what . . .

ANYA. You're at it again, uncle!

BARBARA. Why don't you hold your tongue, uncle?

FIRS [*angrily*]. Leoníd Andréyevitch!

GAYEF. I'm coming; I'm coming. Now go to bed. Off two cushions in the middle pocket! I start another life! . . .

[*Exit, with* FIRS *hobbling after him.*]

ANYA. Now my mind is at rest. I don't want to go to Yaroslav; I don't like grandmamma; but my mind is at rest, thanks to Uncle Leoníd. [*She sits down.*]

BARBARA. Time for bed. I'm off. Whilst you were away there's been a scandal. You know that nobody lives in the old servants' quarters except the old people, Ephim, Pauline, Evstignéy and old Karp. Well, they took to having in all sorts of queer fish to sleep there with them. I didn't say a word. But at last I heard they had spread a report that I had given orders that they were to have nothing but peas to eat; out of stinginess, you understand? It was all Evstignéy's doing. 'Very well,' I said to myself, 'you wait a bit.' So I sent for Evstignéy. [*Yawning.*] He comes. 'Now then, Evstignéy.' I said, 'you old imbecile, how do you dare . . .' [*Looking at* ANYA.] Anya, Anya! [*A pause.*] She's asleep. [*Taking* ANYA's *arm.*] Let's go to bed. Come along. [*Leading her away.*] Sleep on, my little one! Come along; come along! [*They go towards* ANYA's *room. In the distance beyond the orchard a shepherd plays his pipe.*

TROPHIMOF *crosses the stage and, seeing* BARBARA *and* ANYA, *stops.*]
'Sh! She's asleep, she's asleep! Come along, my love.

ANYA [*drowsily*]. I'm so tired! Listen to the bells! Uncle, dear uncle! Mamma! Uncle!

BARBARA. Come along, my love! Come along.

[*Exeunt* BARBARA *and* ANYA *to the bedroom.*]

TROPHIMOF [*with emotion*]. My sunshine! My spring!

CURTAIN

Act II

In the open fields; an old crooked half-ruined shrine. Near it a well; big stones, apparently old tombstones; an old bench. Road to the estate beyond. On one side rise dark poplar trees. Beyond them begins the cherry orchard. In the distance a row of telegraph poles, and, far away on the horizon, the dim outlines of a big town, visible only in fine, clear weather. It is near sunset.

CHARLOTTE, YASHA and DUNYASHA sit on the bench. EPHIKHODOF stands by them and plays on a guitar; they meditate. CHARLOTTE wears an old peaked cap. She has taken a gun from off her shoulders and is mending the buckle of the strap.

CHARLOTTE [*thoughtfully*]. I have no proper passport. I don't know how old I am; I always feel I am still young. When I was a little girl my father and mother used to go about from one country fair to another, giving performances, and very good ones too. I used to do the *salto mortale* and all sorts of tricks. When papa and mamma died an old German lady adopted me and educated me. Good! When I grew up I became a governess. But where I come from and who I am, I haven't a notion. Who my parents were—very likely they weren't married—I don't know. [*Taking a cucumber from her pocket and beginning to eat it.*] I don't know anything about it. [*A pause.*] I long to talk so, and I have no one to talk to, I have no friends or relations.

EPHIKHODOF [*playing on the guitar and singing*].

> 'What is the noisy world to me?
> Oh, what are friends and foes?'

How sweet it is to play upon a mandoline!

DUNYASHA. That's a guitar, not a mandoline. [*She looks at herself in a hand-glass and powders her face.*]

EPHIKHODOF. For the madman who loves, it is a mandoline. [*Singing.*]

17

'Oh, that my heart were cheered
By the warmth of requited love.'

[YASHA *joins in.*]

CHARLOTTE. How badly these people do sing! Foo! Like jackals howling!

DUNYASHA [*to* YASHA]. What happiness it must be to live abroad!

YASHA. Of course it is; I quite agree with you. [*He yawns and lights a cigar.*]

EPHIKHODOF. It stands to reason. Everything abroad has attained a certain culmination.

YASHA. That's right.

EPHIKHODOF. I am a man of cultivation; I have studied various remarkable books, but I cannot fathom the direction of my preferences; do I want to live or do I want to shoot myself, so to speak? But in order to be ready for all contingencies, I always carry a revolver in my pocket. Here it is. [*Showing revolver.*]

CHARLOTTE. That's done. I'm off. [*Slinging the rifle over her shoulder.*] You're a clever fellow, Ephikhódof, and very alarming. Women must fall madly in love with you. Brrr! [*Going.*] These clever people are all so stupid; I have no one to talk to. I am always alone, always alone; I have no friends or relations, and who I am, or why I exist, is a mystery.

[*Exit slowly.*]

EPHIKHODOF. Strictly speaking, without touching upon other matters, I must protest *inter alia* that destiny treats me with the utmost rigour, as a tempest might treat a small ship. If I labour under a misapprehension, how is it that when I woke up this morning, behold, so to speak, I perceived sitting on my chest a spider of praeternatural dimensions, like that [*indicating with both hands*]? And if I go to take a draught of quass, I am sure to find something of the most indelicate character, in the nature of a cockroach. [*A pause.*] Have you read Buckle? [*A pause.*] [*To* DUNYASHA.] I should like to trouble you, Avdótya Fyódorovna, for a momentary interview.

DUNYASHA. Talk away.

EPHIKHODOF. I should prefer to conduct it *tête-à-tête*. [*Sighing.*]

DUNYASHA [*confused*]. Very well, only first please fetch me my cloak. It's by the cupboard. It's rather damp here.

EPHIKHODOF. Very well, mademoiselle. I will go and fetch it, mademoiselle. Now I know what to do with my revolver.

[*Takes his guitar and exit, playing.*]

YASHA. Twenty-two misfortunes! Between you and me, he's a stupid fellow. [*Yawning.*]

DUNYASHA. Heaven help him, he'll shoot himself! [*A pause.*] I have grown so nervous, I am always in a twitter. I was quite a little girl when they took me into the household, and now I have got quite disused to common life, and my hands are as white as white, like a lady's. I have grown so refined, so delicate and genteel, I am afraid of everything. I'm always frightened. And if you deceive me, Yásha, I don't know what will happen to my nerves.

YASHA [*kissing her*]. You little cucumber! Of course every girl ought to behave herself properly; there's nothing I dislike as much as when girls aren't proper in their behaviour.

DUNYASHA. I've fallen dreadfully in love with you. You're so educated; you can talk about anything! [*A pause.*]

YASHA [*yawning*]. Yes. . . . The way I look at it is this; if a girl falls in love with anybody, then I call her immoral. [*A pause.*] How pleasant it is to smoke one's cigar in the open air. [*Listening.*] There's someone coming. It's the missis and the rest of 'em. . . . [DUNYASHA *embraces him hastily.*] Go towards the house as if you'd just been for a bathe. Go by this path or else they'll meet you and think that I've been walking out with you. I can't stand that sort of thing.

DUNYASHA [*coughing softly*]. Your cigar has given me a headache.

[*Exit* DUNYASHA.]

[YASHA *remains sitting by the shrine. Enter* MADAME RANEVSKY, GAYEF *and* LOPAKHIN.]

LOPAKHIN. You must make up your minds once and for all. Time waits for no man. The question is perfectly simple. Are you going to let off the land for villas or not? Answer in one word; yes or no. Only one word!

MADAME RANEVSKY. Who's smoking horrible cigars here? [*She sits down.*]

GAYEF. How handy it is now they've built that railway. [*Sitting.*] We've been into town for lunch and back again. . . . Red in the middle! I must just go up to the house and have a game.

MADAME RANEVSKY. There's no hurry.

LOPAKHIN. Only one word—yes or no! [*Entreatingly.*] Come, answer the question!

GAYEF [*yawning*]. Who's that?

MADAME RANEVSKY [*looking into her purse*]. I had a lot of money yesterday but there's hardly any left now. Poor Barbara tries to save money by feeding us all on milk soup; the old people in the kitchen get nothing but peas, and yet I go squandering aimlessly. . . . [*Dropping her purse and scattering gold coins; vexed.*] There, I've dropped it all!

YASHA. Allow me, I'll pick it up. [*Collecting the coins.*]

MADAME RANEVSKY. Yes, please do, Yásha! Whatever made me go into town for lunch? I hate your horrid restaurant with the organ and the tablecloths all smelling of soap. Why do you drink so much, Leoníd? Why do you eat so much? Why do you talk so much? You talked too much at the restaurant again, and most unsuitably, about the seventies, and the decadents. And to whom? Fancy talking about decadents to the waiters!

LOPAKHIN. Quite true.

GAYEF [*with a gesture*]. I'm incorrigible, that's plain. [*Irritably to* YASHA.] What do you keep dodging about in front of me for?

YASHA [*laughing*]. I can't hear your voice without laughing.

GAYEF [*to* MADAME RANEVSKY]. Either he or I . . .

MADAME RANEVSKY. Go away, Yásha; run along.

YASHA [*handing* MADAME RANEVSKY *her purse*]. I'll go at once. [*Restraining his laughter with difficulty.*] This very minute.

[*Exit* YASHA.]

LOPAKHIN. Derigánof, the millionaire, wants to buy your property. They say he'll come to the auction himself.

MADAME RANEVSKY. How did you hear?

LOPAKHIN. I was told so in town.

GAYEF. Our aunt at Yaroslav has promised to send something; but I don't know when, or how much.

LOPAKHIN. How much will she send? Ten thousand pounds? Twenty thousand pounds?

MADAME RANEVSKY. Oh, come . . . A thousand or fifteen hundred at the most.

LOPAKHIN. Excuse me, but in all my life I never met anybody so frivolous as you two, so crazy and unbusinesslike! I tell you in plain Russian your property is going to be sold, and you don't seem to understand what I say.

MADAME RANEVSKY. Well, what are we to do? Tell us what you want us to do.

LOPAKHIN. Don't I tell you every day? Every day I say the same thing over and over again. You must lease off the cherry orchard and the rest of the estate for villas; you must do it at once, this very moment; the auction will be on you in two twos! Try and understand. Once you make up your mind there are to be villas, you can get all the money you want, and you're saved.

MADAME RANEVSKY. Villas and villa residents, oh, please, . . . it's so vulgar!

GAYEF. I quite agree with you.

LOPAKHIN. I shall either cry, or scream, or faint. I can't stand it! You'll be the death of me. [*To* GAYEF.] You're an old woman!

GAYEF. Who's that?

LOPAKHIN. You're an old woman! [*Going.*]

MADAME RANEVSKY [*frightened*]. No, don't go. Stay here, there's a dear! Perhaps we shall think of some way.

LOPAKHIN. What's the good of thinking!

MADAME RANEVSKY. Please don't go; I want you. At any rate it's gayer when you're here. [*A pause.*] I keep expecting something to happen, as if the house were going to tumble down about our ears.

GAYEF [*in deep abstraction*]. Off the cushion on the corner; double into the middle pocket. . . .

MADAME RANEVSKY. We have been very, very sinful!

LOPAKHIN. You! What sins have you committed?

GAYEF [*eating candy*]. They say I've devoured all my substance in sugar candy. [*Laughing.*]

MADAME RANEVSKY. Oh, the sins that I have committed . . . I've always squandered money at random like a madwoman; I married a man who made nothing but debts. My husband drank himself to death on champagne; he was a fearful drinker. Then for my sins I fell in love and went off with another man; and immediately—that was my first punishment—a blow full on the head . . . here, in this very river . . . my little boy was drowned; and I went abroad, right, right away, never to come back any more, never to see this river again. . . . I shut my eyes and ran, like a mad thing, and *he* came after me, pitiless and cruel. I bought a villa at Mentone, because he fell ill there, and for three years I knew no rest day or night; the sick man tormented and wore down my soul. Then, last year, when my villa was sold to pay my debts, I went off to Paris, and he came and robbed me of everything, left me and took up with another woman, and I tried to poison myself. . . . It was all so stupid, so humiliating. . . . Then suddenly I longed to be back in Russia, in my own country, with my little girl. . . . [*Wiping away her tears.*] Lord, Lord, be merciful to me; forgive my sins! Do not punish me any more! [*Taking a telegram from her pocket.*] I got this to-day from Paris. . . . He asks to be forgiven, begs me to go back. . . . [*Tearing up the telegram.*] Isn't that music that I hear? [*Listening.*]

GAYEF. That's our famous Jewish band. You remember? Four fiddles, a flute and a double bass.

MADAME RANEVSKY. Does it still exist? We must make them come up some time; we'll have a dance.

LOPAKHIN [*listening*]. I don't hear anything. [*Singing softly.*]

> 'The Germans for a fee will turn
> A Russ into a Frenchman.'

[*Laughing.*] I saw a very funny piece at the theatre last night; awfully funny!

MADAME RANEVSKY. It probably wasn't a bit funny. You people ought to go and see plays; you ought to try to see yourselves; to see what a dull life you lead, and how much too much you talk.

LOPAKHIN. Quite right. To tell the honest truth, our life's an imbecile affair. [*A pause.*] My papa was a peasant, an idiot; he understood nothing; he taught me nothing; all he did was to beat me when he was drunk, with a walking-stick. As a matter of fact I'm just as big a blockhead and idiot as he was. I never did any lessons; my handwriting's abominable; I write so badly I'm ashamed before people; like a pig.

MADAME RANEVSKY. You ought to get married.

LOPAKHIN. Yes, that's true.

MADAME RANEVSKY. Why not marry Barbara? She's a nice girl.

LOPAKHIN. Yes.

MADAME RANEVSKY. She's a nice straightforward creature; works all day; and what's most important, she loves you. You've been fond of her for a long time.

LOPAKHIN. Well, why not? I'm quite willing. She's a very nice girl. [*A pause.*]

GAYEF. I've been offered a place in a bank. Six hundred pounds a year. Do you hear?

MADAME RANEVSKY. You in a bank! Stay where you are.

[*Enter* FIRS *carrying an overcoat.*]

FIRS [*to* GAYEF]. Put this on, please, master; it's getting damp.

GAYEF [*putting on the coat*]. What a plague you are, Firs!

FIRS. What's the use. . . . You went off and never told me. [*Examining his clothes.*]

MADAME RANEVSKY. How old you've got, Firs!

FIRS. I beg your pardon?

LOPAKHIN. She says how old you've got!

FIRS. I've been alive a long time. When they found me a wife, your father wasn't even born yet. [*Laughing.*] And when the Liberation came I was already chief valet. But I wouldn't have any Liberation then; I stayed with the master. [*A pause.*] I remember how happy everybody was, but why they were happy they didn't know themselves.

LOPAKHIN. It was fine before then. Anyway they used to flog 'em.

FIRS [*mishearing him*]. I should think so! The peasants minded the masters, and the masters minded the peasants, but now it's all higgledy-piggledy; you can't make head or tail of it.

GAYEF. Shut up, Firs. I must go into town again to-morrow. I've been promised an introduction to a general who'll lend money on a bill.

LOPAKHIN. You'll do no good. You won't even pay the interest; set your mind at ease about that.

MADAME RANEVSKY [*to* LOPAKHIN]. He's only talking nonsense. There's no such general at all.

[*Enter* TROPHIMOF, ANYA *and* BARBARA.]

GAYEF. Here come the others.

ANYA. Here's the mamma.

MADAME RANEVSKY [*tenderly*]. Come along, come along, . . . my little ones. . . . [*Embracing* ANYA *and* BARBARA.] If only you knew how much I love you both! Sit beside me . . . there, like that. [*Everyone sits.*]

LOPAKHIN. The Perpetual Student's always among the girls.

TROPHIMOF. It's no affair of yours.

LOPAKHIN. He's nearly fifty and still a student.

TROPHIMOF. Stop your idiotic jokes!

LOPAKHIN. What are you losing your temper for, silly?

TROPHIMOF. Why can't you leave me alone?

LOPAKHIN [*laughing*]. I should like to know what your opinion is of me?

TROPHIMOF. My opinion of you, Yermolái Alexéyitch, is this. You're a rich man; you'll soon be a millionaire. Just as a beast of prey which devours everything that comes in its way is necessary for the conversion of matter, so you are necessary too.

[*All laugh.*]

BARBARA. Tell us something about the planets, Peter, instead.

MADAME RANEVSKY. No. Let's go on with the conversation we were having yesterday.

TROPHIMOF. What about?

GAYEF. About the proud man.

TROPHIMOF. We had a long talk yesterday, but we didn't come to any conclusion. There is something mystical in the proud man in the sense in which you use the words. You may be right from your point of view, but, if we look at it simple-mindedly, what room is there for pride? Is there any sense in it, when man is so poorly constructed from the physiological point of view, when the vast majority of us are so gross and stupid and profoundly unhappy? We must give up admiring ourselves. The only thing to do is to work.

GAYEF. We shall die all the same.

TROPHIMOF. Who knows? And what does it mean, to die? Perhaps man has a hundred senses, and when he dies only the five senses that we know perish with him, and the other ninety-five remain alive.

MADAME RANEVSKY. How clever you are, Peter.

LOPAKHIN [*ironically*]. Oh, extraordinary!

TROPHIMOF. Mankind marches forward, perfecting its strength. Everything that is unattainable for us now will one day be near and clear; but we must work; we must help with all our force those who seek for truth. At present only a few men work in Russia. The vast majority of the educated people that I know seek after nothing, do nothing, and are as yet incapable of work. They call themselves the 'Intelligentsia,' they say 'thou' and 'thee' to the servants, they treat the peasants like animals, learn nothing, read nothing serious, do absolutely nothing, only talk about science, and understand little or nothing about art. They are all serious; they all have solemn faces; they only discuss important subjects; they philosophise; but meanwhile the vast majority of us, ninety-nine per cent., live like savages; at the least thing they curse and punch people's heads; they eat like beasts and sleep in dirt and bad air; there are bugs everywhere, evil smells, damp and moral degradation. . . . It's plain that all our clever conversations are only meant to distract our own attention and other people's. Show me where those crèches are, that they're always talking so much about; or those reading-rooms. They are only things people write about in novels; they don't really exist at all. Nothing exists but dirt, vulgarity and Asiatic ways. I am afraid of solemn faces; I dislike them; I am afraid of solemn conversations. Let us rather hold our tongues.

LOPAKHIN. Do you know, I get up at five every morning. I work from morning till night; I am always handling my own money or other people's, and I see the sort of men there are about me. One only has to begin to do anything to see how few honest and decent people there are. Sometimes, as I lie awake in bed, I think: 'O Lord, you have given us mighty forests, boundless fields and immeasurable horizons, and we, living in their midst, ought really to be giants.'

MADAME RANEVSKY. Oh dear, you want giants! They are all very well in fairy stories; but in real life they are rather alarming. [EPHIKHODOF *passes at the back of the scene, playing on his guitar.*] [*Pensively.*] There goes Ephikhódof.

ANYA [*pensively*]. There goes Ephikhódof.

GAYEF. The sun has set.

TROPHIMOF. Yes.

GAYEF [*as if declaiming, but not loud*]. O Nature, wonderful Nature, you glow with eternal light; beautiful and indifferent, you whom we call our mother, uniting in yourself both life and death, you animate and you destroy. . . .

BARBARA [*entreatingly*]. Uncle!

ANYA. You're at it again, uncle!

TROPHIMOF. You'd far better double the red into the middle pocket.

GAYEF. I'll hold my tongue! I'll hold my tongue!

[*They all sit pensively. Silence reigns, broken only by the mumbling of old* FIRS. *Suddenly a distant sound is heard as if from the sky, the sound of a string breaking, dying away, melancholy.*]

MADAME RANEVSKY. What's that?

LOPAKHIN. I don't know. It's a lifting-tub given way somewhere away in the mines. It must be a long way off.

GAYEF. Perhaps it's some sort of bird . . . a heron, or something.

TROPHIMOF. Or an owl. . . .

MADAME RANEVSKY [*shuddering*]. There's something uncanny about it!

FIRS. The same thing happened before the great misfortune: the owl screeched and the samovar kept humming.

GAYEF. What great misfortune?

FIRS. The Liberation. [*A pause.*]

MADAME RANEVSKY. Come, everyone, let's go in; it's getting late. [*To* ANYA.] You've tears in your eyes. What is it, little one? [*Embracing her.*]

ANYA. Nothing, mamma. I'm all right.

TROPHIMOF. There's someone coming.

[*A Tramp appears in a torn white-peaked cap and overcoat. He is slightly drunk.*]

TRAMP. Excuse me, but can I go through this way straight to the station?

GAYEF. Certainly. Follow this path.

TRAMP. I am uncommonly obliged to you, sir. [*Coughing.*] We're having lovely weather. [*Declaiming.*] 'Brother, my suffering brother' . . . 'Come forth to the Volga. Who moans?' . . . [*To* BARBARA.] Mademoiselle, please spare a sixpence for a hungry fellow-countryman.

[BARBARA, *frightened, screams.*]

LOPAKHIN [*angrily*]. There's a decency for even indecency to observe.

MADAME RANEVSKY. Take this; here you are. [*Fumbling in her purse.*] I haven't any silver. . . . Never mind, take this sovereign.

TRAMP. I am uncommonly obliged to you, madam.

[*Exit* TRAMP. *Laughter.*]

BARBARA [*frightened*]. I'm going! I'm going! Oh, mamma, there's nothing for the servants to eat at home, and you've gone and given this man a sovereign.

MADAME RANEVSKY. What's to be done with your stupid old mother? I'll give you up everything I have when I get back. Yermolái Alexéyitch, lend me some more money.

LOPAKHIN. Very good.

MADAME RANEVSKY. Come along, everyone; it's time to go in. We've settled all about your marriage between us, Barbara. I wish you joy.

BARBARA [*through her tears*]. You mustn't joke about such things, mamma.

LOPAKHIN. Amelia, get thee to a nunnery, go!

GAYEF. My hands are all trembling; it's ages since I had a game of billiards.

LOPAKHIN. Amelia, nymphlet, in thine orisons remember me.

MADAME RANEVSKY. Come along. It's nearly supper-time.

BARBARA. How he frightened me! My heart is simply throbbing.

LOPAKHIN. Allow me to remind you, the cherry orchard is to be sold on the twenty-second of August. Bear that in mind; bear that in mind!

[*Exeunt omnes except* TROPHIMOF *and* ANYA.]

ANYA [*laughing*]. Many thanks to the Tramp for frightening Barbara; at last we are alone.

TROPHIMOF. Barbara's afraid we shall go and fall in love with each other. Day after day she never leaves us alone. With her narrow mind she cannot understand that we are above love. To avoid everything petty, everything illusory, everything that prevents one from being free and happy, that is the whole meaning and purpose of our life. Forward! We march on irresistibly towards that bright star which burns far, far before us! Forward! Don't tarry, comrades!

ANYA [*clasping her hands*]. What beautiful things you say! [*A pause.*] Isn't it enchanting here to-day!

TROPHIMOF. Yes, it's wonderful weather.

ANYA. What have you done to me, Peter? Why is it that I no longer love the cherry orchard as I did? I used to love it so tenderly; I thought there was no better place on earth than our garden.

TROPHIMOF. All Russia is our garden. The earth is great and beautiful; it is full of wonderful places. [*A pause.*] Think, Anya, your grandfather, your great-grandfather and all your ancestors were serf-owners, owners of living souls. Do not human spirits look out at you from every tree in the orchard, from every leaf and every stem? Do you not hear human voices? . . . Oh! it is terrible. Your orchard frightens me. When I walk through it in the evening or at night, the rugged bark on the trees glows with a dim light, and the cherry trees seem to see all that happened a hundred and two hundred years ago in painful and oppressive dreams. Well, well, we have fallen at least two hundred years behind the times. We have achieved nothing at all as yet; we have not made up our minds how we stand with the past; we only philosophise, complain of boredom, or drink vodka. It is so plain that, before we can live in the present, we must first redeem the past, and have done with it; and it is only by suffering that we can redeem it, only by strenuous, unremitting toil. Understand that, Anya.

ANYA. The house we live in has long since ceased to be our house; and I shall go away, I give you my word.

TROPHIMOF. If you have the household keys, throw them in the well and go away. Be free, be free as the wind.

ANYA [*enthusiastically*]. How beautifully you put it!

TROPHIMOF. Believe what I say, Anya; believe what I say. I'm not thirty yet; I am still young, still a student; but what I have been through! I am hungry as the winter; I am sick, anxious, poor as a beggar. Fate has tossed me hither and thither; I have been everywhere, everywhere. But wherever I have been, every minute, day and night, my soul has been full of mysterious anticipations. I feel the approach of happiness; Anya; I see it coming. . . .

ANYA [*pensively*]. The moon is rising.

[EPHIKHODOF *is heard still playing the same sad tune on his guitar. The moon rises. Somewhere beyond the poplar trees,* BARBARA *is heard calling for* ANYA: '*Anya, where are you?*']

TROPHIMOF. Yes, the moon is rising. [*A pause.*] There it is, there is happiness; it is coming towards us, nearer and nearer; I can hear the sound of its footsteps. . . . And if we do not see it, if we do not know it, what does it matter? Others will see it.

BARBARA [*without*]. Anya? Where are you?

TROPHIMOF. There's Barbara again! [*Angrily.*] It really is too bad!

ANYA. Never mind. Let us go down to the river. It's lovely there.

TROPHIMOF. Come on!

[*Exeunt* ANYA *and* TROPHIMOF.]

BARBARA [*without*]. Anya! Anya!

CURTAIN

Act III

A *sitting-room separated by an arch from a big drawing-room behind. Chandelier lighted. The Jewish band mentioned in Act II is heard playing on the landing. Evening. In the drawing-room they are dancing the grand rond.* SIMEONOF-PISHTCHIK *is heard crying: 'Promenade à une paire!'*

The dancers come down into the sitting-room. The first pair consists of PISHTCHIK *and* CHARLOTTE; *the second of* TROPHIMOF *and* MADAME RANEVSKY; *the third of* ANYA *and the* POST OFFICE OFFICIAL; *the fourth of* BARBARA *and the* STATION-MASTER, *etc., etc.* BARBARA *is crying softly and wipes away the tears as she dances. In the last pair comes* DUNYASHA. *They cross the sitting-room.*

PISHTCHIK. Grand rond, balancez. . . . Les cavaliers à genou et remerciez vos dames.

[FIRS *in evening dress carries seltzer water across on a tray.* PISHTCHIK *and* TROPHIMOF *come down into the sitting-room.*]

PISHTCHIK. I am a full-blooded man; I've had two strokes already; it's hard work dancing, but, as the saying goes: 'If you run with the pack, bark or no, but anyway wag your tail.' I'm as strong as a horse. My old father, who was fond of his joke, rest his soul, used to say, talking of our pedigree, that the ancient stock of the Simeónof-Píshtchiks was descended from that very horse that Caligula made a senator. . . . [*Sitting.*] But the worst of it is, I've got no money. A hungry dog believes in nothing but meat. [*Snoring and waking up again at once.*] I'm just the same. . . . It's nothing but money, money, with me.

TROPHIMOF. Yes, it's quite true, there is something horselike about your build.

PISHTCHIK. Well, well . . . a horse is a jolly creature . . . you can sell a horse.

28

[*A sound of billiards being played in the next room.* BARBARA *appears in the drawing-room beyond the arch.*]

TROPHIMOF [*teasing her*]. Madame Lopákhin! Madame Lopákhin!
BARBARA [*angrily*]. Mouldy gentleman!
TROPHIMOF. Yes, I'm a mouldy gentleman, and I'm proud of it.
BARBARA [*bitterly*]. We've hired the band, but where's the money to pay for it?

[*Exit* BARBARA.]

TROPHIMOF [*to* PISHTCHIK]. If the energy which you have spent in the course of your whole life in looking for money to pay the interest on your loans had been diverted to some other purpose, you would have had enough of it, I dare say, to turn the world upside down.
PISHTCHIK. Nietzsche, the philosopher, a very remarkable man, very famous, a man of gigantic intellect, says in his works that it's quite right to forge banknotes.
TROPHIMOF. What, have you read Nietzsche?
PISHTCHIK. Well . . . Dáshenka told me. . . . But I'm in such a hole, I'd forge 'em for two-pence. I've got to pay thirty-one pounds the day after to-morrow. . . . I've got thirteen pounds already. [*Feeling his pockets; alarmed.*] My money's gone! I've lost my money! [*Crying.*] Where's my money got to? [*Joyfully.*] Here it is, inside the lining. . . . It's thrown me all in a perspiration.

[*Enter* MADAME RANEVSKY *and* CHARLOTTE.]

MADAME RANEVSKY [*humming a lezginka*]. Why is Leoníd so long? What can he be doing in the town? [*To* DUNYASHA.] Dunyásha, ask the musicians if they'll have some tea.
TROPHIMOF. The sale did not come off, in all probability.
MADAME RANEVSKY. It was a stupid day for the musicians to come; it was a stupid day to have this dance. . . . Well, well, it doesn't matter. . . .
[*She sits down and sings softly to herself.*]
CHARLOTTE [*giving* PISHTCHIK *a pack of cards*]. Here is a pack of cards. Think of any card you like.
PISHTCHIK. I've thought of one.
CHARLOTTE. Now shuffle the pack. That's all right. Give them here, O most worthy Mr. Píshtchik. Ein, zwei, drei! Now look and you'll find it in your side pocket.
PISHTCHIK [*taking a card from his side pocket*]. The Eight of Spades. You're perfectly right. [*Astonished.*] Well, I never!
CHARLOTTE [*holding the pack on the palm of her hand, to* TROPHIMOF]. Say quickly, what's the top card?

TROPHIMOF. Well, say the Queen of Spades.

CHARLOTTE. Right! [*To* PISHTCHIK.] Now then, what's the top card?

PISHTCHIK. Ace of Hearts.

CHARLOTTE. Right! [*She claps her hands; the pack of cards disappears.*] What a beautiful day we've been having.

[*A mysterious female* VOICE *answers her as if from under the floor:* 'Yes, indeed, a charming day, mademoiselle.']

CHARLOTTE. You are my beautiful ideal.

THE VOICE. '*I think you also ferry peautiful, mademoiselle.*'

STATION-MASTER [*applauding*]. Bravo, Miss Ventriloquist!

PISHTCHIK [*astonished*]. Well, I never! Bewitching Charlotte Ivánovna, I'm head over ears in love with you.

CHARLOTTE. In love! [*Shrugging her shoulders.*] Are you capable of love? Guter Mensch, aber schlechter Musikant!

TROPHIMOF [*slapping* PISHTCHIK *on the shoulder*]. You old horse!

CHARLOTTE. Now attention, please; one more trick. [*Taking a shawl from a chair.*] Now here's a shawl, and a very pretty shawl; I'm going to sell this very pretty shawl. [*Shaking it.*] Who'll buy? who'll buy?

PISHTCHIK [*astonished*]. Well, I never!

CHARLOTTE. Ein, zwei, drei! [*She lifts the shawl quickly; behind it stands* ANYA, *who drops a curtsy, runs to her mother, kisses her, then runs up into the drawing-room amid general applause.*]

MADAME RANEVSKY [*applauding*]. Bravo! bravo!

CHARLOTTE. Once more. Ein, zwei, drei! [*She lifts up the shawl; behind it stands* BARBARA, *bowing.*]

PISHTCHIK [*astonished*]. Well, I never!

CHARLOTTE. That's all. [*She throws the shawl over* PISHTCHIK, *makes a curtsy and runs up into the drawing-room.*]

PISHTCHIK [*hurrying after her*]. You little rascal . . . there's a girl for you, there's a girl. . . .

[*Exit.*]

MADAME RANEVSKY. And still no sign of Leoníd. What he's doing in the town so long, I can't understand. It must be all over by now; the property's sold; or the auction never came off; why does he keep me in suspense so long?

BARBARA [*trying to soothe her*]. Uncle has bought it, I am sure of that.

TROPHIMOF [*mockingly*]. Of course he has!

BARBARA. Grannie sent him a power of attorney to buy it in her name and transfer the mortgage. She's done it for Anya's sake. I'm perfectly sure that Heaven will help us and uncle will buy it.

MADAME RANEVSKY. Your Yaroslav grannie sent fifteen hundred pounds to buy the property in her name—she doesn't trust us—but it wouldn't be enough even to pay the interest. [*Covering her face with her hands.*] My fate is being decided to-day, my fate. . . .

TROPHIMOF [*teasing* BARBARA]. Madame Lopákhin!

BARBARA [*angrily*]. Perpetual Student! He's been sent down twice from the University.

MADAME RANEVSKY. Why do you get angry, Barbara? He calls you Madame Lopákhin for fun. Why not? You can marry Lopákhin if you like; he's a nice, interesting man; you needn't if you don't; nobody wants to force you, my pet.

BARBARA. I take it very seriously, mamma, I must confess. He's a nice man and I like him.

MADAME RANEVSKY. Then marry him. There's no good putting it off that I can see.

BARBARA. But, mamma, I can't propose to him myself. For two whole years everybody's been talking about him to me, everyone; but he either says nothing or makes a joke of it. I quite understand. He's making money; he's always busy; he can't be bothered with me. If I only had some money, even a little, even ten pounds, I would give everything up and go right away. I would go into a nunnery.

TROPHIMOF [*mockingly*]. What bliss!

BARBARA [*to* TROPHIMOF]. A student ought to be intelligent. [*In a gentler voice, crying.*] How ugly you've grown, Peter; how old you've grown! [*She stops crying; to* MADAME RANEVSKY.] But I can't live without work, mamma. I must have something to do every minute of the day.

[*Enter* YASHA.]

YASHA [*trying not to laugh*]. Ephikhódof has broken a billiard cue.

[*Exit* YASHA.]

BARBARA. What's Ephikhódof doing here? Who gave him leave to play billiards? I don't understand these people.

[*Exit* BARBARA.]

MADAME RANEVSKY. Don't tease her, Peter. Don't you see that she's unhappy enough already?

TROPHIMOF. I wish she wouldn't be so fussy, always meddling in other people's affairs. The whole summer she's given me and Anya no peace; she is afraid we'll work up a romance between us. What business is it of hers? I'm sure I never gave her any grounds; I'm not likely to be so commonplace. We are above love!

MADAME RANEVSKY. Then I suppose I must be beneath love. [*Deeply agitated.*] Why doesn't Leoníd come? Oh, if only I knew whether the property's sold or not! It seems such an impossible disaster, that I don't know what to think. . . . I'm bewildered. . . . I shall burst out screaming, I shall do something idiotic. Save me, Peter; say something to me, say something. . . .

TROPHIMOF. Whether the property is sold to-day or whether it's not sold, surely it's all one? It's all over with it long ago; there's no turning back, the path is overgrown. Be calm, dear Lyubóf Andréyevna. You mustn't deceive yourself any longer; for once you must look the truth straight in the face.

MADAME RANEVSKY. What truth? You can see what's truth, and what's untruth, but I seem to have lost the power of vision; I see nothing. You settle every important question so boldly; but tell me, Peter, isn't that because you're young, because you have never solved any question of your own as yet by suffering? You look boldly ahead; isn't it only that you don't see or divine anything terrible in the future; because life is still hidden from your young eyes? You are bolder, honester, deeper than we are, but reflect, show me just a finger's breadth of consideration, take pity on me. Don't you see? I was born here, my father and mother lived here, and my grandfather; I love this house; without the cherry orchard my life has no meaning for me, and if it *must* be sold, then for heaven's sake sell me too! [*Embracing* TROPHIMOF *and kissing him on the forehead.*] My little boy was drowned here. [*Crying.*] Be gentle with me, dear, kind Peter.

TROPHIMOF. You know I sympathise with all my heart.

MADAME RANEVSKY. Yes, yes, but you ought to say it somehow differently. [*Taking out her handkerchief and dropping a telegram.*] I am so wretched to-day, you can't imagine! All this noise jars on me, my heart jumps at every sound. I tremble all over; but I can't shut myself up; I am afraid of the silence when I'm alone. Don't be hard on me, Peter; I love you like a son. I would gladly let Anya marry you, I swear it; but you must work, Peter; you must get your degree. You do nothing; Fate tosses you about from place to place; and that's not right. It's true what I say, isn't it? And you must do something to your beard to make it grow better. [*Laughing.*] I can't help laughing at you.

TROPHIMOF [*picking up the telegram*]. I don't wish to be an Adonis.

MADAME RANEVSKY. It's a telegram from Paris. I get them every day. One came yesterday, another to-day. That savage is ill again; he's in a bad way. . . . He asks me to forgive him, he begs me to come; and I really ought to go to Paris and be with him. You look at me sternly; but what am I to do, Peter? What am I to do? He's ill, he's lonely, he's unhappy. Who is to look after him? Who is to keep him from doing stupid things? Who is to give him his medicine when it's time? After all, why should I be ashamed to say it? I love him, that's plain. I love him, I love him. . . . My love is like a stone tied round my neck; it's dragging me down to the bottom; but I love my stone. I can't live without it. [*Squeezing* TROPHIMOF's *hand*.] Don't think ill of me, Peter; don't say anything! Don't say anything!

TROPHIMOF [*crying*]. Forgive my bluntness, for heaven's sake; but the man has simply robbed you.

MADAME RANEVSKY. No, no, no! [*Stopping her ears*.] You mustn't say that!

TROPHIMOF. He's a rascal; everybody sees it but yourself; he's a petty rascal, a ne'er-do-well. . . .

MADAME RANEVSKY [*angry but restrained*]. You're twenty-six or twenty-seven, and you're still a Lower School boy!

TROPHIMOF. Who cares?

MADAME RANEVSKY. You ought to be a man by now; at your age you ought to understand people who love. You ought to love someone yourself, you ought to be in love! [*Angrily*.] Yes, yes! It's not purity with you; it's simply you're a smug, a figure of fun, a freak. . . .

TROPHIMOF [*horrified*]. What does she say?

MADAME RANEVSKY. 'I am above love!' You're not above love; you're simply what Firs calls a 'job-lot.' At your age you ought to be ashamed not to have a mistress!

TROPHIMOF [*aghast*]. This is awful! What does she say? [*Going quickly up into the drawing-room, clasping his head with his hands*.] This is something awful! I can't stand it; I'm off . . . [*Exit, but returns at once*.] All is over between us!

[*Exit to landing*.]

MADAME RANEVSKY [*calling after him*]. Stop, Peter! Don't be ridiculous; I was only joking! Peter!

[TROPHIMOF *is heard on the landing going quickly down the stairs, and suddenly falling down them with a crash.* ANYA *and* BARBARA *scream. A moment later the sound of laughter*.]

MADAME RANEVSKY. What has happened?

[ANYA *runs in*.]

ANYA [*laughing*]. Peter's tumbled downstairs. [*She runs out again*.]
MADAME RANEVSKY. What a ridiculous fellow he is!

[*The* STATION-MASTER *stands in the middle of the drawing-room behind the arch and recites Alexey Tolstoy's poem, 'The Sinner.' Everybody stops to listen, but after a few lines the sound of a waltz is heard from the landing and he breaks off. All dance.* TROPHIMOF, ANYA, BARBARA *and* MADAME RANEVSKY *enter from the landing.*]

MADAME RANEVSKY. Come, Peter, come, you pure spirit. . . . I beg your pardon. Let's have a dance. [*She dances with* TROPHIMOF. ANYA *and* BARBARA *dance.*]

[*Enter* FIRS, *and stands his walking-stick by the side door. Enter* YASHA *by the drawing-room; he stands looking at the dancers.*]

YASHA. Well, grandfather?

FIRS. I'm not feeling well. In the old days it was generals and barons and admirals that danced at our dances, but now we send for the Postmaster and the Station-Master, and even they make a favour of coming. I'm sort of weak all over. The old master, their grandfather, used to give us all sealing wax, when we had anything the matter. I've taken sealing wax every day for twenty years and more. Perhaps that's why I'm still alive.

YASHA. I'm sick of you, grandfather. [*Yawning.*] I wish you'd die and have done with it.

FIRS. Ah! you . . . job-lot! [*He mumbles to himself.*]

[TROPHIMOF *and* MADAME RANEVSKY *dance beyond the arch and down into the sitting-room.*]

MADAME RANEVSKY. Merci. I'll sit down. [*Sitting.*] I'm tired.

[*Enter* ANYA.]

ANYA [*agitated*]. There was somebody in the kitchen just now saying that the cherry orchard was sold to-day.

MADAME RANEVSKY. Sold? Who to?

ANYA. He didn't say who to. He's gone. [*She dances with* TROPHIMOF. *Both dance up into the drawing-room.*]

YASHA. It was some old fellow chattering; a stranger.

FIRS. And still Leoníd Andréyitch doesn't come. He's wearing his light overcoat *demi-saison*; he'll catch cold as like as not. Ah, young wood, green wood!

MADAME RANEVSKY. This is killing me. Yásha, go and find out who it was sold to.

YASHA. Why, he's gone long ago, the old man. [*Laughs.*]

MADAME RANEVSKY [*vexed*]. What are you laughing at? What are you glad about?

YASHA. He's a ridiculous fellow, is Ephikhódof. Nothing in him. Twenty-two misfortunes!

MADAME RANEVSKY. Firs, if the property is sold, where will you go to?

FIRS. Wherever you tell me, there I'll go.

MADAME RANEVSKY. Why do you look like that? Are you ill? You ought to be in bed.

FIRS [*ironically*]. Oh yes, I'll go to bed, and who'll hand the things around, who'll give orders? I've the whole house on my hands.

YASHA. Lyubóf Andréyevna! Let me ask a favour of you; be so kind; if you go to Paris again, take me with you, I beseech you. It's absolutely impossible for me to stay here. [*Looking about; sotto voce.*] What's the use of talking? You can see for yourself this is a barbarous country; the people have no morals; and the boredom! The food in the kitchen is something shocking, and on the top of it old Firs goes about mumbling irrelevant nonsense. Take me back with you; be so kind!

[*Enter* PISHTCHIK.]

PISHTCHIK. May I have the pleasure . . . a bit of a waltz, charming lady? [MADAME RANEVSKY *takes his arm*.] All the same, enchanting lady, you must let me have eighteen pounds. [*Dancing.*] Let me have . . . eighteen pounds.

[*Exeunt dancing through the arch.*]

YASHA [*singing to himself*].

> 'Oh, wilt thou understand
> The turmoil of my soul?'

[*Beyond the arch appears a figure in grey tall hat and check trousers, jumping and waving its arms. Cries of 'Bravo, Charlotte Ivánovna.'*]

DUNYASHA [*stopping to powder her face*]. Mamselle Anya tells me I'm to dance; there are so many gentlemen and so few ladies. But dancing makes me giddy and makes my heart beat, Firs Nikoláyevitch; and just now the gentleman from the post office said something so nice to me, oh, so nice! It quite took my breath away. [*The music stops.*]

FIRS. What did he say to you?

DUNYASHA. He said, 'You are like a flower.'

YASHA [*yawning*]. Cad!

[*Exit* YASHA.]

DUNYASHA. Like a flower! I am so ladylike and refined, I dote on compliments.

FIRS. You'll come to a bad end.

[*Enter* EPHIKHODOF.]

EPHIKHODOF. You are not pleased to see me, Avdótya Fyódorovna, no more than if I were some sort of insect. [*Sighing.*] Ah! Life! Life!

DUNYASHA. What do you want?

EPHIKHODOF. Undoubtedly perhaps you are right. [*Sighing.*] But of course, if one regards it, so to speak, from the point of view, if I may allow myself the expression, and with apologies for my frankness, you have finally reduced me to a state of mind. I quite appreciate my destiny; every day some misfortune happens to me, and I have long since grown accustomed to it, and face my fortune with a smile. You have passed your word to me, and although I . . .

DUNYASHA. Let us talk of this another time, if you please; but now leave me in peace. I am busy meditating. [*Playing with her fan.*]

EPHIKHODOF. Every day some misfortune befalls me, and yet, if I may venture to say so, I meet them with smiles and even laughter.

[*Enter* BARBARA *from the drawing-room.*]

BARBARA [*to* EPHIKHODOF]. Haven't you gone yet, Simeon? You seem to pay no attention to what you're told. [*To* DUNYASHA.] You get out of here, Dunyásha. [*To* EPHIKHODOF.] First you play billiards and break a cue, and then you march about the drawing-room as if you were a guest!

EPHIKHODOF. Allow me to inform you that it's not your place to call me to account.

BARBARA. I'm not calling you to account; I'm merely talking to you. All you can do is to walk about from one place to another, without ever doing a stroke of work; and why on earth we keep a clerk at all heaven only knows.

EPHIKHODOF [*offended*]. Whether I work, or whether I walk, or whether I eat, or whether I play billiards is a question to be decided only by my elders and people who understand.

BARBARA [*furious*]. How dare you talk to me like that! How dare you! I don't understand things, don't I? You clear out of here this minute! Do you hear me? This minute!

EPHIKHODOF [*flinching*]. I must beg you to express yourself in genteeler language.

BARBARA [*beside herself*]. You clear out this instant second! Out you go! [*Following him as he retreats towards the door.*] Twenty-two misfortunes! Make yourself scarce! Get out of my sight!

[*Exit* EPHIKHODOF.]

EPHIKHODOF [*without*]. I shall lodge a complaint against you.

BARBARA. What! You're coming back, are you? [*Seizing the walking-stick left at the door by* FIRS.] Come on! Come on! Come on! I'll teach you! Are you coming? Are you coming? Then take that. [*She slashes with the stick.*]

[*Enter* LOPAKHIN.]

LOPAKHIN. Many thanks; much obliged.

BARBARA [*still angry, but ironical*]. Sorry!

LOPAKHIN. Don't mention it. I'm very grateful for your warm reception.

BARBARA. It's not worth thanking me for. [*She walks away, then looks round and asks in a gentle voice.*] I didn't hurt you?

LOPAKHIN. Oh, no, nothing to matter. I shall have a bump like a goose's egg, that's all.

[*Voices from the drawing-room:* 'Lopákhin has arrived! Yermolái Alexéyitch!']

PISHTCHIK. Let my eyes see him, let my ears hear him! [*He and* LOPAKHIN *kiss.*] You smell of brandy, old man. We're having a high time, too.

[*Enter* MADAME RANEVSKY.]

MADAME RANEVSKY. Is it you, Yermolái Alexéyitch? Why have you been so long? Where is Leoníd?

LOPAKHIN. Leoníd Andréyitch came back with me. He's just coming.

MADAME RANEVSKY [*agitated*]. What happened? Did the sale come off? Tell me, tell me!

LOPAKHIN [*embarrassed, afraid of showing his pleasure.*] The sale was all over by four o'clock. We missed the train and had to wait till half-past eight. [*Sighing heavily.*] Ouf! I'm rather giddy. . . .

[*Enter* GAYEF. *In one hand he carries parcels; with the other he wipes away his tears.*]

MADAME RANEVSKY. What happened, Lénya? Come, Lénya! [*Impatiently, crying.*] Be quick, be quick, for heaven's sake!

GAYEF [*answering her only with an up and down gesture of the hand; to* FIRS, *crying*]. Here, take these. . . . Here are some anchovies and Black Sea herrings. I've had nothing to eat all day. Lord, what I've been through! [*Through the open door of the billiard-room comes the click of the billiard balls and* YASHA'S *voice:* 'Seven, eighteen!' GAYEF'S *expression changes; he stops crying.*] I'm frightfully tired. Come and help me change, Firs. [*He goes up through the drawing-room,* FIRS *following.*]

PISHTCHIK. What about the sale? Come on, tell us all about it.

MADAME RANEVSKY. Was the cherry orchard sold?

LOPAKHIN. Yes.

MADAME RANEVSKY. Who bought it?

LOPAKHIN. I did. [*A pause.* MADAME RANEVSKY *is overwhelmed at the news. She would fall to the ground but for the chair and table by her.* BARBARA *takes the keys from her belt, throws them on the floor in the middle of the sitting-room, and exit.*] I bought it. Wait a bit; don't hurry me; my head's in a whirl; I can't speak. . . . [*Laughing.*] When we got to the sale, Deriganof was there already. Leoníd Andréyitch had only fifteen hundred pounds, and Deriganof bid three thousand more than the mortgage right away. When I saw how things stood, I went for him and bid four thousand. He said four thousand five hundred. I said five thousand five hundred. He went up by five hundreds, you see, and I went up by thousands. . . . Well, it was soon over. I bid nine thousand more than the mortgage, and got it; and now the cherry orchard is mine! Mine! [*Laughing.*] Heaven's alive! Just think of it! The cherry orchard is mine! Tell me that I'm drunk; tell me that I'm off my head; tell me that it's all a dream! . . . [*Stamping his feet.*] Don't laugh at me! If only my father and my grandfather could rise from their graves and see the whole affair, how their Yermolái, their flogged and ignorant Yermolái, who used to run about barefooted in the winter, how this same Yermolái had bought a property that hasn't its equal for beauty anywhere in the whole world! I have bought the property where my father and grandfather were slaves, where they weren't even allowed into the kitchen. I'm asleep, it's only a vision, it isn't real. . . . 'Tis the fruit of imagination, wrapped in the mists of ignorance. [*Picking up the keys and smiling affectionately.*] She's thrown down her keys; she wants to show that she's no longer mistress here. . . . [*Jingling them together.*] Well, well, what's the odds? [*The musicians are heard tuning up.*] Hey, musicians, play! I want to hear you. Come everyone and see Yermolái Lopákhin lay his axe to the cherry orchard, come and see the trees fall down! We'll fill the place with villas; our grandsons and great-grandsons shall see a new life here. . . . Strike up, music! [*The band plays.* MADAME RANEVSKY *sinks into a chair and weeps bitterly.*] [*Reproachfully.*] Oh, why, why didn't you listen to me? You can't put the clock back now, poor dear. [*Crying.*] Oh, that all this were past and over! Oh, that our unhappy topsy-turvy life were changed!

PISHTCHIK [*taking him by the arm, sotto voce*]. She's crying. Let's go into the drawing-room and leave her alone to . . . Come on. [*Taking him by the arm, and going up towards the drawing-room.*]

LOPAKHIN. What's up? Play your best, musicians! Let everything be as I want. [*Ironically.*] Here comes the new squire, the owner of the cherry orchard! [*Knocking up by accident against a table and nearly throwing down the candelabra.*] Never mind, I can pay for everything!

[*Exit with* PISHTCHIK. *Nobody remains in the drawing-room or sitting-room except* MADAME RANEVSKY, *who sits huddled together, weeping bitterly. The band plays softly. Enter* ANYA *and* TROPHIMOF *quickly.* ANYA *goes to her mother and kneels before her.* TROPHIMOF *stands in the entry to the drawing-room.*]

ANYA. Mamma! Are you crying, mamma? My dear, good, sweet mamma! Darling, I love you! I bless you! The cherry orchard is sold; it's gone; it's quite true, it's quite true. But don't cry, mamma, you've still got life before you, you've still got your pure and lovely soul. Come with me, darling; come away from here. We'll plant a new garden, still lovelier than this. You will see it and understand, and happiness, deep, tranquil happiness will sink down on your soul, like the sun at eventide, and you'll smile, mamma. Come, darling, come with me!

CURTAIN

Act IV

Same scene as Act I. There are no window-curtains, no pictures. The little furniture left is stacked in a corner, as if for sale. A feeling of emptiness. By the door to the hall and at the back of the scene are piled portmanteaux, bundles, etc. The door is open and the voices of BARBARA *and* ANYA *are audible.*

[LOPAKHIN *stands waiting.* YASHA *holds a tray with small tumblers full of champagne.* EPHIKHODOF *is tying up a box in the hall. A distant murmur of voices behind the scene; the* PEASANTS *have come to say good-bye.*]

GAYEF [*without*]. Thank you, my lads, thank you.

YASHA. The common people have come to say good-bye. I'll tell you what I think, Yermolái Alexéyitch; they're good fellows but rather stupid.

[*The murmur of voices dies away. Enter* MADAME RANEVSKY *and* GAYEF *from the hall. She is not crying, but she is pale, her face twitches, she cannot speak.*]

GAYEF. You gave them your purse, Lyuba. That was wrong, very wrong!

MADAME RANEVSKY. I couldn't help it, I couldn't help it!

[*Exeunt both.*]

LOPAKHIN [*calling after them through the doorway*]. Please come here! Won't you come here? Just a glass to say good-bye. I forgot to bring any from town, and could only raise one bottle at the station. Come along. [*A pause.*] What, won't you have any? [*Returning from the door.*] If I'd known, I wouldn't have bought it. I shan't have any either. [YASHA *sets the tray down carefully on a chair.*] Drink it yourself, Yásha.

YASHA. Here's to our departure! Good luck to them that stay! [*Drinking.*] This isn't real champagne, you take my word for it.

40

LOPAKHIN. Sixteen shillings a bottle. [*A pause.*] It's devilish cold in here.

YASHA. The fires weren't lighted to-day; we're all going away. [*He laughs.*]

LOPAKHIN. What are you laughing for?

YASHA. Just pleasure.

LOPAKHIN. Here we are in October, but it's as calm and sunny as summer. Good building weather. [*Looking at his watch and speaking off.*] Don't forget that there's only forty-seven minutes before the train goes. You must start for the station in twenty minutes. Make haste.

[*Enter* TROPHIMOF *in an overcoat, from out of doors.*]

TROPHIMOF. I think it's time we were off. The carriages are round. What the deuce has become of my goloshes? I've lost 'em. [*Calling off.*] Anya, my goloshes have disappeared. I can't find them anywhere!

LOPAKHIN. I've got to go to Kharkof. I'll start in the same train with you. I'm going to spend the winter in Kharkof. I've been loafing about all this time with you people, eating my head off for want of work. I can't live without work, I don't know what to do with my hands; they dangle about as if they didn't belong to me.

TROPHIMOF. Well, we're going now, and you'll be able to get back to your beneficent labours.

LOPAKHIN. Have a glass.

TROPHIMOF. Not for me.

LOPAKHIN. Well, so you're off to Moscow?

TROPHIMOF. Yes, I'll see them into the town, and go on to Moscow to-morrow.

LOPAKHIN. Well, well. . . . I suppose the professors haven't started their lectures yet; they're waiting till you arrive.

TROPHIMOF. It is no affair of yours.

LOPAKHIN. How many years have you been up at the University?

TROPHIMOF. Try and think of some new joke; this one's getting a bit flat. [*Looking for his goloshes.*] Look here, I dare say we shan't meet again, so let me give you a bit of advice as a keepsake: Don't flap your hands about! Get out of the habit of flapping. Building villas, prophesying that villa residents will turn into small freeholders, all that sort of thing is flapping too. Well, when all's said and done, I like you. You have thin, delicate, artist fingers; you have a delicate, artist soul.

LOPAKHIN [*embracing him*]. Good-bye, old chap. Thank you for everything. Take some money off me for the journey if you want it.

TROPHIMOF. What for? I don't want it.

LOPAKHIN. But you haven't got any.

TROPHIMOF. Yes, I have. Many thanks. I got some for a translation. Here it is, in my pocket. [*Anxiously.*] I can't find my goloshes anywhere!

BARBARA [*from the next room*]. Here, take your garbage away! [*She throws a pair of goloshes on the stage.*]

TROPHIMOF. What are you so cross about, Barbara? Humph! . . . But those aren't *my* goloshes!

LOPAKHIN. In the spring I sowed three thousand acres of poppy and I have cleared four thousand pounds net profit. When my poppies were in flower, what a picture they made! So you see, I cleared four thousand pounds; and I wanted to lend you a bit because I've got it to spare. What's the good of being stuck up? I'm a peasant. . . . As man to man. . . .

TROPHIMOF. Your father was a peasant; mine was a chemist; it doesn't prove anything. [LOPAKHIN *takes out his pocket-book with paper money.*] Shut up, shut up. . . . If you offered me twenty thousand pounds I would not take it. I am a free man; nothing that you value so highly, all of you, rich and poor, has the smallest power over me; it's like thistledown floating on the wind. I can do without you; I can go past you; I'm strong and proud. Mankind marches forward to the highest truth, to the highest happiness possible on earth, and I march in the foremost ranks.

LOPAKHIN. Will you get there?

TROPHIMOF. Yes. [*A pause.*] I will get there myself or I will show others the way.

[*The sound of axes hewing is heard in the distance.*]

LOPAKHIN. Well, good-bye, old chap; it is time to start. Here we stand swaggering to each other, and life goes by all the time without heeding us. When I work for hours without getting tired, I get easy in my mind and I seem to know why I exist. But God alone knows what most of the people in Russia were born for. . . . Well, who cares? It doesn't affect the circulation of work. They say Leoníd Andréyitch has got a place; he's going to be in a bank and get six hundred pounds a year. . . . He won't sit it out, he's too lazy.

ANYA [*in the doorway*]. Mamma says, will you stop cutting down the orchard till she has gone.

TROPHIMOF. Really, haven't you got tact enough for that?

[*Exit* TROPHIMOF *by the hall.*]

LOPAKHIN. Of course, I'll stop them at once. What fools they are!

[*Exit after* TROPHIMOF.]

ANYA. Has Firs been sent to the hospital?

YASHA. I told 'em this morning. They're sure to have sent him.

ANYA [*to* EPHIKHODOF, *who crosses*]. Simeon Panteléyitch, please find out if Firs has been sent to the hospital.

YASHA [*offended*]. I told George this morning. What's the good of asking a dozen times?

EPHIKHODOF. Our centenarian friend, in my conclusive opinion, is hardly worth tinkering; it's time he was dispatched to his forefathers. I can only say I envy him. [*Putting down a portmanteau on a bandbox and crushing it flat.*] There you are! I knew how it would be!

[*Exit.*]

YASHA [*jeering*]. Twenty-two misfortunes.

BARBARA [*without*]. Has Firs been sent to the hospital?

ANYA. Yes.

BARBARA. Why didn't they take the note to the doctor?

ANYA. We must send it after them.

[*Exit* ANYA.]

BARBARA [*from the next room*]. Where's Yásha? Tell him his mother is here. She wants to say good-bye to him.

YASHA [*with a gesture of impatience*]. It's enough to try the patience of a saint!

[DUNYASHA *has been busying herself with the luggage. Seeing* YASHA *alone, she approaches him.*]

DUNYASHA. You might just look once at me, Yásha. You are going away, you are leaving me. [*Crying and throwing her arms round his neck.*]

YASHA. What's the good of crying? [*Drinking champagne.*] In six days I shall be back in Paris. To-morrow we take the express, off we go, and that's the last of us! I can hardly believe it's true. Vive la France! This place don't suit me. I can't bear it . . . it can't be helped. I have had enough barbarism; I'm fed up. [*Drinking champagne.*] What's the good of crying? You be a good girl, and you'll have no call to cry.

DUNYASHA [*powdering her face and looking into a glass*]. Write me a letter from Paris. I've been so fond of you, Yásha, ever so fond! I am a delicate creature, Yásha.

YASHA. Here's somebody coming. [*He busies himself with the luggage, singing under his breath.*]

[*Enter* MADAME RANEVSKY, GAYEF, ANYA *and* CHARLOTTE.]

GAYEF. We'll have to be off; it's nearly time. [*Looking at* YASHA.] Who is it smells of red herring?

MADAME RANEVSKY. We must take our seats in ten minutes. [*Looking*

round the room.] Good-bye, dear old house, good-bye, grandpapa!
When winter is past and spring comes again, you will be here no more;
they will have pulled you down. Oh, think of all these walls have seen!
[*Kissing* ANYA *passionately.*] My treasure, you look radiant, your eyes
flash like two diamonds. Are you happy? very happy?

ANYA. Very, very happy. We're beginning a new life, mamma.

GAYEF [*gaily*]. She's quite right, everything's all right now. Till the cherry
orchard was sold we were all agitated and miserable; but once the thing
was settled finally and irrevocably, we all calmed down and got jolly
again. I'm a bank clerk now; I'm a financier . . . red in the middle! And
you, Lyuba, whatever you may say, you're looking ever so much better,
not a doubt about it.

MADAME RANEVSKY. Yes, my nerves are better; it's quite true. [*She is
helped on with her hat and coat.*] I sleep well now. Take my things out,
Yásha. We must be off. [*To* ANYA.] We shall soon meet again, darling. . . . I'm off to Paris; I shall live on the money your grandmother
sent from Yaroslav to buy the property. God bless your grandmother!
I'm afraid it won't last long.

ANYA. You'll come back very, very soon, won't you, mamma? I'm going
to work and pass the examination at the Gymnase and get a place and
help you. We'll read all sorts of books together, won't we, mamma?
[*Kissing her mother's hands.*] We'll read in the long autumn evenings,
we'll read heaps of books, and a new, wonderful world will open up
before us. [*Meditating.*] . . . Come back, mamma!

MADAME RANEVSKY. I'll come back, my angel. [*Embracing her.*]

[*Enter* LOPAKHIN. CHARLOTTE *sings softly.*]

GAYEF. Happy Charlotte, she's singing.

CHARLOTTE [*taking a bundle of rugs, like a swaddled baby*]. Hush-
a-bye, baby, on the tree top . . . [*The baby answers, 'Wah, wah.'*]
Hush, my little one, hush, my pretty one! ['*Wah, wah.'*] You'll break
your mother's heart. [*She throws the bundle down on the floor again.*]
Don't forget to find me a new place, please. I can't do without it.

LOPAKHIN. We'll find you a place, Charlotte Ivánovna, don't be afraid.

GAYEF. Everybody's deserting us. Barbara's going. Nobody seems to
want us.

CHARLOTTE. There's nowhere for me to live in the town. I'm obliged to
go. [*Hums a tune.*] What's the odds?

[*Enter* PISHTCHIK.]

LOPAKHIN. Nature's masterpiece!

PISHTCHIK [*panting*]. Oy, oy, let me get my breath again! . . . I'm done
up! . . . My noble friends! . . . Give me some water.

GAYEF. Wants some money, I suppose. No, thank you; I'll keep out of harm's way.

[*Exit.*]

PISHTCHIK. It's ages since I have been here, fairest lady. [*To* LOPAKHIN.] You here? Glad to see you, you man of gigantic intellect. Take this; it's for you. [*Giving* LOPAKHIN *money.*] Forty pounds! I still owe you eighty-four.

LOPAKHIN [*amazed, shrugging his shoulders*]. It's like a thing in a dream! Where did you get it from?

PISHTCHIK. Wait a bit. . . . I'm hot. . . . A most remarkable thing! Some Englishmen came and found some sort of white clay on my land. [*To* MADAME RANEVSKY.] And here's forty pounds for you, lovely, wonderful lady. [*Giving her money.*] The rest another time. [*Drinking water.*] Only just now a young man in the train was saying that some . . . some great philosopher advises us all to jump off roofs. . . . Jump, he says, and there's an end of it. [*With an astonished air.*] Just think of that! More water!

LOPAKHIN. Who were the Englishmen?

PISHTCHIK. I leased them the plot with the clay on it for twenty-four years. But I haven't any time now . . . I must be getting on. I must go to Znoikof's, to Kardamónof's. . . . I owe everybody money. [*Drinking.*] Good-bye to everyone; I'll look in on Thursday.

MADAME RANEVSKY. We're just moving into town, and to-morrow I go abroad.

PISHTCHIK. What! [*Alarmed.*] What are you going into town for? Why, what's happened to the furniture? . . . Trunks? . . . Oh, it's all right. [*Crying.*] It's all right. People of powerful intellect . . . those Englishmen. It's all right. Be happy . . . God be with you . . . it's all right. Everything in this world has come to an end. [*Kissing* MADAME RANEVSKY'S *hand.*] If ever the news reaches you that I have come to an end, give a thought to the old . . . horse, and say, 'Once there lived a certain Simeónof-Píshtchik, Heaven rest his soul.'. . . Remarkable weather we're having. . . . Yes. . . . [*Goes out deeply moved. Returns at once and says from the doorway.*] Dáshenka sent her compliments.

[*Exit.*]

MADAME RANEVSKY. Now we can go. I have only two things on my mind. One is poor old Firs. [*Looking at her watch.*] We can still stay five minutes.

ANYA. Firs has been sent to the hospital already, mamma. Yásha sent him off this morning.

MADAME RANEVSKY. My second anxiety is Barbara. She's used to getting up early and working, and now that she has no work to do she's like a fish out of water. She has grown thin and pale and taken to crying, poor dear. . . . [*A pause.*] You know very well, Yermolái Alexéyitch, I always hoped . . . to see her married to you, and as far as I can see, you're looking out for a wife. [*She whispers to* ANYA, *who nods to* CHARLOTTE, *and both exeunt.*] She loves you; you like her; and I can't make out why you seem to fight shy of each other. I don't understand it.

LOPAKHIN. I don't understand it either, to tell you the truth. It all seems so odd. If there's still time, I'll do it this moment. Let's get it over and have done with it; without you there, I feel as if I should never propose to her.

MADAME RANEVSKY. A capital idea! After all, it doesn't take more than a minute. I'll call her at once.

LOPAKHIN. And here's the champagne all ready. [*Looking at the glasses.*] Empty; someone's drunk it. [YASHA *coughs.*] That's what they call lapping it up and no mistake!

MADAME RANEVSKY [*animated*]. Capital! We'll all go away. . . . *Allez,* Yásha. I'll call her. [*At the door.*] Barbara, leave all that and come here. Come along!

[*Exeunt* MADAME RANEVSKY *and* YASHA.]

LOPAKHIN [*looking at his watch*]. Yes.

[*A pause. A stifled laugh behind the door; whispering; at last enter* BARBARA.]

BARBARA [*examining the luggage*]. Very odd; I can't find it anywhere . . .
LOPAKHIN. What are you looking for?
BARBARA. I packed it myself, and can't remember. [*A pause.*]
LOPAKHIN. Where are you going to-day, Varvára Mikháilovna?
BARBARA. Me? I'm going to the Ragulins'. I'm engaged to go and keep house for them, to be housekeeper or whatever it is.
LOPAKHIN. Oh, at Yáshnevo? That's about fifty miles from here. [*A pause.*] Well, so life in this house is over now.
BARBARA [*looking at the luggage*]. Wherever can it be? Perhaps I put it in the trunk. . . . Yes, life here is over now; there won't be any more . . .
LOPAKHIN. And I'm off to Kharkof at once . . . by the same train. A lot of business to do. I'm leaving Ephikhódof to look after this place. I've taken him on.
BARBARA. Have you?
LOPAKHIN. At this time last year snow was falling already, if you remember; but now it's fine and sunny. Still, it's cold for all that. Three degrees of frost.

BARBARA. Were there? I didn't look. [*A pause.*] Besides, the thermometer's broken. [*A pause.*]

A VOICE [*at the outer door*]. Yermolái Alexéyitch!

LOPAKHIN [*as if he had only been waiting to be called*]. I'm just coming! [*Exit* LOPAKHIN *quickly.*]

[BARBARA *sits on the floor, puts her head on a bundle and sobs softly. The door opens and* MADAME RANEVSKY *comes in cautiously.*]

MADAME RANEVSKY. Well? [*A pause.*] We must be off.

BARBARA [*no longer crying, wiping her eyes*]. Yes, it's time, mamma. I shall get to the Ragulins' all right to-day, so long as I don't miss the train.

MADAME RANEVSKY [*calling off*]. Put on your things, Anya.

[*Enter* ANYA, *then* GAYEF *and* CHARLOTTE. GAYEF *wears a warm overcoat with a hood. The servants and drivers come in.* EPHIKHODOF *busies himself about the luggage.*]

MADAME RANEVSKY. Now we can start on our journey.

ANYA [*delighted*]. We can start on our journey!

GAYEF. My friends, my dear, beloved friends! Now that I am leaving this house for ever, can I keep silence? Can I refrain from expressing those emotions which fill my whole being at such a moment?

ANYA [*pleadingly*]. Uncle!

BARBARA. Uncle, what's the good?

GAYEF [*sadly*]. Double the red in the middle pocket. I'll hold my tongue.

[*Enter* TROPHIMOF, *then* LOPAKHIN.]

TROPHIMOF. Come along, it's time to start.

LOPAKHIN. Ephikhódof, my coat.

MADAME RANEVSKY. I must sit here another minute. It's just as if I had never noticed before what the walls and ceilings of the house were like. I look at them hungrily, with such tender love. . . .

GAYEF. I remember, when I was six years old, how I sat in this window on Trinity Sunday, and watched father starting out for church.

MADAME RANEVSKY. Has everything been cleared out?

LOPAKHIN. Apparently everything. [*To* EPHIKHODOF, *putting on his overcoat.*] See that everything's in order, Ephikhódof.

EPHIKHODOF [*in a hoarse voice*]. You trust me, Yermolái Alexéyitch.

LOPAKHIN. What's up with your voice?

EPHIKHODOF. I was just having a drink of water. I swallowed something.

YASHA [*contemptuously*]. Cad!

MADAME RANEVSKY. We're going, and not a soul will be left here.

LOPAKHIN. Until the spring.

[BARBARA *pulls an umbrella out of a bundle of rugs, as if she were brandishing it to strike.* LOPAKHIN *pretends to be frightened.*]

BARBARA. Don't be so silly! I never thought of such a thing.

TROPHIMOF. Come, we'd better go and get in. It's time to start. The train will be in immediately.

BARBARA. There are your goloshes, Peter, by that portmanteau. [*Crying.*] What dirty old things they are!

TROPHIMOF [*putting on his goloshes*]. Come along.

GAYEF [*much moved, afraid of crying*]. The train . . . the station . . . double the red in the middle; doublette to pot the white in the corner. . . .

MADAME RANEVSKY. Come on!

LOPAKHIN. Is everyone here? No one left in there? [*Locking the door.*] There are things stacked in there; I must lock them up. Come on!

ANYA. Good-bye, house! good-bye, old life!

TROPHIMOF. Welcome, new life!

[*Exit with* ANYA. BARBARA *looks round the room, and exit slowly.* Exeunt YASHA, *and* CHARLOTTE *with her dog.*]

LOPAKHIN. Till the spring, then. Go on, everybody. So-long!

[*Exit.* MADAME RANEVSKY *and* GAYEF *remain alone. They seem to have been waiting for this, throw their arms round each other's necks and sob restrainedly and gently, afraid of being overheard.*]

GAYEF [*in despair*]. My sister! my sister!

MADAME RANEVSKY. Oh, my dear, sweet lovely orchard! My life, my youth, my happiness, farewell! Farewell!

ANYA [*calling gaily, without*]. Mamma!

TROPHIMOF [*gay and excited*]. Aoo!

MADAME RANEVSKY. One last look at the walls and the windows. . . . Our dear mother used to walk up and down this room.

GAYEF. My sister! my sister!

ANYA [*without*]. Aoo!

MADAME RANEVSKY. We're coming. [*Exeunt.*]

[*The stage is empty. One hears all the doors being locked, and the carriages driving away. All is quiet. Amid the silence the thud of the axes on the trees echoes sad and lonely. The sound of footsteps.* FIRS *appears in the doorway* R. *He is dressed, as always, in his long coat and white waistcoat; he wears slippers. He is ill.*]

FIRS [*going to the door L. and trying the handle*]. Locked. They've gone. [*Sitting on the sofa.*] They've forgotten me. Never mind! I'll sit here. Leoníd Andréyitch is sure to have put on his cloth coat instead of his fur. [*He sighs anxiously.*] He hadn't me to see. Young wood, green wood! [*He mumbles something incomprehensible.*] Life has gone by as if I'd never lived. [*Lying down.*] I'll lie down. There's no strength left in you; there's nothing, nothing. Ah, you . . . job-lot!

[*He lies motionless. A distant sound is heard, as if from the sky, the sound of a string breaking, dying away, melancholy. Silence ensues, broken only by the stroke of the axe on the trees far away in the cherry orchard.*]

CURTAIN

DOVER · THRIFT · EDITIONS

All books complete and unabridged. All 5³/₁₆″ × 8¹/₄″, paperbound.
Just $1.00–$2.00 in U.S.A.

POETRY

DOVER BEACH AND OTHER POEMS, Matthew Arnold. 112pp. 28037-3 $1.00

BHAGAVADGITA, Bhagavadgita. 112pp. 27782-8 $1.00

SONGS OF INNOCENCE AND SONGS OF EXPERIENCE, William Blake. 64pp. 27051-3 $1.00

SONNETS FROM THE PORTUGUESE AND OTHER POEMS, Elizabeth Barrett Browning. 64pp. 27052-1 $1.00

MY LAST DUCHESS AND OTHER POEMS, Robert Browning. 128pp. 27783-6 $1.00

POEMS AND SONGS, Robert Burns. 96pp. 26863-2 $1.00

SELECTED POEMS, George Gordon, Lord Byron. 112pp. 27784-4 $1.00

THE RIME OF THE ANCIENT MARINER AND OTHER POEMS, Samuel Taylor Coleridge. 80pp. 27266-4 $1.00

SELECTED POEMS, Emily Dickinson. 64pp. 26466-1 $1.00

SELECTED POEMS, John Donne. 96pp. 27788-7 $1.00

THE RUBÁIYÁT OF OMAR KHAYYÁM: FIRST AND FIFTH EDITIONS, Edward FitzGerald. 64pp. 26467-X $1.00

A BOY'S WILL AND NORTH OF BOSTON, Robert Frost. 112pp. (Available in U.S. only.) 26866-7 $1.00

THE ROAD NOT TAKEN AND OTHER POEMS, Robert Frost. 64pp. (Available in U.S. only) 27550-7 $1.00

A SHROPSHIRE LAD, A. E. Housman. 64pp. 26468-8 $1.00

LYRIC POEMS, John Keats. 80pp. 26871-3 $1.00

THE BOOK OF PSALMS, King James Bible. 128pp. 27541-8 $1.00

GUNGA DIN AND OTHER FAVORITE POEMS, Rudyard Kipling. 80pp. 26471-8 $1.00

THE CONGO AND OTHER POEMS, Vachel Lindsay. 96pp. 27272-9 $1.00

FAVORITE POEMS, Henry Wadsworth Longfellow. 96pp. 27273-7 $1.00

SPOON RIVER ANTHOLOGY, Edgar Lee Masters. 144pp. 27275-3 $1.00

RENASCENCE AND OTHER POEMS, Edna St. Vincent Millay. 64pp. (Available in U.S. only.) 26873-X $1.00

SELECTED POEMS, John Milton. 128pp. 27554-X $1.00

GREAT SONNETS, Paul Negri (ed.). 96pp. 28052-7 $1.00

THE RAVEN AND OTHER FAVORITE POEMS, Edgar Allan Poe. 64pp. 26685-0 $1.00

ESSAY ON MAN AND OTHER POEMS, Alexander Pope. 128pp. 28053-5 $1.00

GOBLIN MARKET AND OTHER POEMS, Christina Rossetti. 64pp. 28055-1 $1.00

CHICAGO POEMS, Carl Sandburg. 80pp. 28057-8 $1.00

THE SHOOTING OF DAN MCGREW AND OTHER POEMS, Robert Service. 96pp. 27556-6 $1.00

COMPLETE SONGS FROM THE PLAYS, William Shakespeare. 80pp. 27801-8 $1.00

COMPLETE SONNETS, William Shakespeare. 80pp. 26686-9 $1.00

SELECTED POEMS, Percy Bysshe Shelley. 128pp. 27558-2 $1.00

SELECTED POEMS, Alfred Lord Tennyson. 112pp. 27282-6 $1.00

CHRISTMAS CAROLS: COMPLETE VERSES, Shane Weller (ed.). 64pp. 27397-0 $1.00

DOVER · THRIFT · EDITIONS

All books complete and unabridged. All 5³⁄₁₆″ × 8¹⁄₄″, paperbound. Just $1.00–$2.00 in U.S.A.

POETRY (continued)

GREAT LOVE POEMS, Shane Weller (ed.). 128pp. 27284-2 $1.00

SELECTED POEMS, Walt Whitman. 128pp. 26878-0 $1.00

THE BALLAD OF READING GAOL AND OTHER POEMS, Oscar Wilde. 64pp. 27072-6 $1.00

FAVORITE POEMS, William Wordsworth. 80pp. 27073-4 $1.00

EARLY POEMS, William Butler Yeats. 128pp. 27808-5 $1.00

FICTION

FLATLAND: A ROMANCE OF MANY DIMENSIONS, Edwin A. Abbott. 96pp. 27263-X $1.00

BEOWULF, Beowulf (trans. by R. K. Gordon). 64pp. 27264-8 $1.00

CIVIL WAR STORIES, Ambrose Bierce. 128pp. 28038-1 $1.00

ALICE'S ADVENTURES IN WONDERLAND, Lewis Carroll. 96pp. 27543-4 $1.00

O PIONEERS!, Willa Cather. 128pp. 27785-2 $1.00

FIVE GREAT SHORT STORIES, Anton Chekhov. 96pp. 26463-7 $1.00

FAVORITE FATHER BROWN STORIES, G. K. Chesterton. 96pp. 27545-0 $1.00

THE AWAKENING, Kate Chopin. 128pp. 27786-0 $1.00

HEART OF DARKNESS, Joseph Conrad. 80pp. 26464-5 $1.00

THE SECRET SHARER AND OTHER STORIES, Joseph Conrad. 128pp. 27546-9 $1.00

THE OPEN BOAT AND OTHER STORIES, Stephen Crane. 128pp. 27547-7 $1.00

THE RED BADGE OF COURAGE, Stephen Crane. 112pp. 26465-3 $1.00

A CHRISTMAS CAROL, Charles Dickens. 80pp. 26865-9 $1.00

THE CRICKET ON THE HEARTH AND OTHER CHRISTMAS STORIES, Charles Dickens. 128pp. 28039-X $1.00

NOTES FROM THE UNDERGROUND, Fyodor Dostoyevsky. 96pp. 27053-X $1.00

SIX GREAT SHERLOCK HOLMES STORIES, Sir Arthur Conan Doyle. 112pp. 27055-6 $1.00

WHERE ANGELS FEAR TO TREAD, E. M. Forster. 128pp. (Available in U.S. only) 27791-7 $1.00

THE OVERCOAT AND OTHER SHORT STORIES, Nikolai Gogol. 112pp. 27057-2 $1.00

GREAT GHOST STORIES, John Grafton (ed.). 112pp. 27270-2 $1.00

THE LUCK OF ROARING CAMP AND OTHER SHORT STORIES, Bret Harte. 96pp. 27271-0 $1.00

THE SCARLET LETTER, Nathaniel Hawthorne. 192pp. 28048-9 $2.00

YOUNG GOODMAN BROWN AND OTHER SHORT STORIES, Nathaniel Hawthorne. 128pp. 27060-2 $1.00

THE GIFT OF THE MAGI AND OTHER SHORT STORIES, O. Henry. 96pp. 27061-0 $1.00

THE NUTCRACKER AND THE GOLDEN POT, E. T. A. Hoffmann. 128pp. 27806-9 $1.00

THE BEAST IN THE JUNGLE AND OTHER STORIES, Henry James. 128pp. 27552-3 $1.00

THE TURN OF THE SCREW, Henry James. 96pp. 26684-2 $1.00

DUBLINERS, James Joyce. 160pp. 26870-5 $1.00

A PORTRAIT OF THE ARTIST AS A YOUNG MAN, James Joyce. 192pp. 28050-0 $2.00

DOVER · THRIFT · EDITIONS

All books complete and unabridged. All 5³⁄₁₆″ × 8¼″, paperbound.
Just $1.00–$2.00 in U.S.A.

FICTION (continued)

THE MAN WHO WOULD BE KING AND OTHER STORIES, Rudyard Kipling. 128pp. 28051-9 $1.00

SELECTED SHORT STORIES, D. H. Lawrence. 128pp. 27794-1 $1.00

GREEN TEA AND OTHER GHOST STORIES, J. Sheridan LeFanu. 96pp. 27795-X $1.00

THE CALL OF THE WILD, Jack London. 64pp. 26472-6 $1.00

FIVE GREAT SHORT STORIES, Jack London. 96pp. 27063-7 $1.00

WHITE FANG, Jack London. 160pp. 26968-X $1.00

THE NECKLACE AND OTHER SHORT STORIES, Guy de Maupassant. 128pp. 27064-5 $1.00

BARTLEBY AND BENITO CERENO, Herman Melville. 112pp. 26473-4 $1.00

THE GOLD-BUG AND OTHER TALES, Edgar Allan Poe. 128pp. 26875-6 $1.00

THE QUEEN OF SPADES AND OTHER STORIES, Alexander Pushkin. 128pp. 28054-3 $1.00

THREE LIVES, Gertrude Stein. 176pp. 28059-4 $2.00

THE STRANGE CASE OF DR. JEKYLL AND MR. HYDE, Robert Louis Stevenson. 64pp. 26688-5 $1.00

TREASURE ISLAND, Robert Louis Stevenson. 160pp. 27559-0 $1.00

THE KREUTZER SONATA AND OTHER SHORT STORIES, Leo Tolstoy. 144pp. 27805-0 $1.00

ADVENTURES OF HUCKLEBERRY FINN, Mark Twain. 224pp. 28061-6 $2.00

THE MYSTERIOUS STRANGER AND OTHER STORIES, Mark Twain. 128pp. 27069-6 $1.00

CANDIDE, Voltaire (François-Marie Arouet). 112pp. 26689-3 $1.00

THE INVISIBLE MAN, H. G. Wells. 112pp. (Available in U.S. only.) 27071-8 $1.00

ETHAN FROME, Edith Wharton. 96pp. 26690-7 $1.00

THE PICTURE OF DORIAN GRAY, Oscar Wilde. 192pp. 27807-7 $1.00

NONFICTION

THE DEVIL'S DICTIONARY, Ambrose Bierce. 144pp. 27542-6 $1.00

THE SOULS OF BLACK FOLK, W. E. B. Du Bois. 176pp. 28041-1 $2.00

SELF-RELIANCE AND OTHER ESSAYS, Ralph Waldo Emerson. 128pp. 27790-9 $1.00

GREAT SPEECHES, Abraham Lincoln. 112pp. 26872-1 $1.00

THE PRINCE, Niccolò Machiavelli. 80pp. 27274-5 $1.00

SYMPOSIUM AND PHAEDRUS, Plato. 96pp. 27798-4 $1.00

THE TRIAL AND DEATH OF SOCRATES: FOUR DIALOGUES, Plato. 128pp. 27066-1 $1.00

CIVIL DISOBEDIENCE AND OTHER ESSAYS, Henry David Thoreau. 96pp. 27563-9 $1.00

THE THEORY OF THE LEISURE CLASS, Thorstein Veblen. 256pp. 28062-4 $2.00

PLAYS

THE CHERRY ORCHARD, Anton Chekhov. 64pp. 26682-6 $1.00

THE THREE SISTERS, Anton Chekhov. 64pp. 27544-2 $1.00

THE WAY OF THE WORLD, William Congreve. 80pp. 27787-9 $1.00

MEDEA, Euripides. 64pp. 27548-5 $1.00

THE MIKADO, William Schwenck Gilbert. 64pp. 27268-0 $1.00